REA

Zoe's Gift

Also by Sheila Hayes

The Carousel Horse

Me and My Mona Lisa Smile

No Autographs, Please

Speaking of Snapdragons

You've Been Away All Summer

Sheila Hayes

LODESTAR BOOKS
Dutton New York

for Chuck

No character in this book is intended to represent any actual person; all the incidents of the story are entirely fictional in nature.

Library of Congress Cataloging-in-Publication Data
Hayes, Sheila.
Zoe's gift / Sheila Hayes.—1st ed.
p. cm.
Summary: While vacationing in England, eleven-year-old Cory meets Zoe, a girl with extrasensory powers, and together they solve a 100-year-old mystery.
ISBN 0-525-67484-5
[1. Extrasensory perception—Fiction. 2. Friendship—Fiction. 3. Mystery and detective stories. 4. England—Fiction.] I. Title.
PZ7.H314874Zo 1994
[Fic]—dc20 93-42621
CIP
AC

Published in the United States by Lodestar Books,
an affiliate of Dutton Children's Books,
a division of Penguin Books USA Inc.,
375 Hudson Street, New York, New York 10014

Published simultaneously in Canada
by McClelland & Stewart, Toronto

Editor: Rosemary Brosnan Designer: Marilyn Granald

Printed in the U.S.A. First Edition
10 9 8 7 6 5 4 3 2 1

I know, I know, you don't believe in that sort of thing. Trust me, neither did I. I live in an apartment on the West Side of Manhattan in New York City, and as far as I know, there have never been any paranormal phenomena going on in *my* building. At least, nobody's mentioned it to me if they've bumped into a ghost putting out the garbage or seen one tying up the elevator because he kept pushing the wrong buttons. Even people who believe in them know that they only hang out in really old places like castles . . . or cemeteries . . . or vaults.

So I'm sure I'd still be a skeptic, too, if we hadn't gone to England last summer. But we *did*—even though I wasn't too keen on the idea—and all this crazy stuff happened that I want to tell you about because I want to make sure I remember it clearly, the way it really was and the way I felt about it right when it was happening. I'm afraid that someday when I'm grown up I might make a joke about it and pretend it wasn't real or that I imagined the whole thing because I have this wild imagination.

But that wasn't it. Honest.

I guess I should begin on the airplane. I was pretty excited because I was flying for the first time. You probably find that hard to believe—eleven years old and she'd never been on an airplane—but that's what happens when you don't have any grandparents living in Florida.

I had pressed my forehead against the window as the plane started to lumber down the runway and now, as it lifted off the ground and I watched the earth fall away beneath us, my stomach did a little flip-flop like it does in elevators sometimes. I couldn't actually see the ground, of course, because it was night, but I could see the lights of Kennedy Airport and the lights on the bridges and the lights on the highways, where the cars looked like little toys being pushed around by kids in preschool. Pretty soon there was a *bing! bing!* and the flight attendant started down the aisle smiling, as if to reassure us that the lift-off had gone just fine and we weren't going to be splashed all over the evening news after all.

As I've already mentioned, we live in New York and both my parents, besides being archaeologists, are academics. That's a fancy word for teachers. Spell that *B-O-R-I-N-G.* They're on the faculty at Columbia, an excellent university, which I'm sure I'll never get into the way my marks are going—no matter how much pull they have.

I think this is the part where I should back up a little and introduce myself.

My name is Cornelia Gales. My mother tried calling me Nell for awhile. Then the kids in school changed it to Corny. Finally we settled on Cory. That's the kind of problem you have when you're named after the famous Cornelia Jessup. Ever hear of her? Of course not. But when my mother says her name, she almost swoons. Cornelia Jessup was my mother's mentor—that's what they call an older person whom you admire a lot and who helps you in your career. She's retired now, but she's really famous among other archaeologists. I even saw her picture in a book once.

Which brings me to how I got dragged along, for the very first time, on one of their "digs."

It was a drizzly morning in May, and my parents were not at all happy. They had their classes to attend, which I had told the school counselor, but she called them and set up the appointment as if it were a matter of life or death. *Guess whose death?*

Studying has never been my thing. I usually do just enough to pass and get promoted to the next grade. This semester I came up with four Cs, one B (that was in English), and an Incomplete. (That was in gym. I never remembered to bring my gym suit.) So the guidance counselor made the phone call.

Ms. Pritchett was my guidance counselor, and she wore lots of makeup and bright colors and jewelry so we'd all think she was cool and not the nerd that most guidance counselors are. But it backfired because we liked the tweedy Mr. Daniels much better, and we all knew that Ms. Pritchett was the biggest nerd in the whole school. And since my school is private, it has a very high nerd quotient.

"Cornelia, when you picture yourself as an adult, what do you see yourself doing?" she asked me when we were all sitting relaxed as tombstones in her office. "What kind of work?" she persisted.

That was easy.

"Anything that's not boring."

"I see. That's interesting. Well, don't you think picking up an odd bit of learning here and there might be a help in this ... uh ... profession?"

"Not really," I said.

"Oh?"

I went on to explain, with the honesty I consider my strongest asset, that I didn't think it was so important to be smart. Not book-learning smart. What I think I will need is a vivid imagination, which I'm trying to develop. That will make whatever I do more fun, right? It didn't work. Three sessions later, she had come to the conclusion that I was so "intimidated by the intellectual superiority" of my parents that I was deliberately underachieving.

In other words, I was rebelling against my parents by becoming your basic moron.

My parents, Barbara and Jeremiah, took it very hard. They've never really pressured me to get good marks. In fact, they never pressure me about anything. Sometimes I kind of wish they would, but my best friend, Diane Freedman, thinks I'm crazy. She says I don't know how lucky I am to have parents who treat me like I'm an adult—my own person is the way she puts it. She thinks it's a hoot that I can call them by their first names if I want to (although most of the time I don't) and that they don't nag me to do my homework. She doesn't realize that they assume I'll do it all on my own because, well, it's just so much *fun.*

Unfortunately, the sessions with the guidance counselor opened their eyes. They became really upset and kept discussing changes that must be made in my life-style, ways that I could be challenged. (That's one of my mother's favorite words.)

Then my father had the brainstorm. Each year my parents go off on an expedition for part of the summer while I get shipped off to Camp Minnehaha in the Catskill Mountains. This year, he says, since they were going to England to work with the famous Cornelia Jessup, maybe I should go with them! Especially since—and here comes the really bad part—old Cornelia has a granddaughter named Zoe, and she's absolutely perfect. She's about my age, but she gets straight As, dresses like Laura Ashley, and listens to Beethoven on those rare occasions when she takes her head out of a book. They didn't actually come out and say so, but I could tell they thought that since Zoe was so *gifted* (another favorite word), she would be a good influence on me.

Right away five-alarmers went off in my head. I like going to camp, and the more I heard about the wonderfully talented Zoe, the more I wanted to barf. So I mounted a protest.

"*Barbara,* I don't think this is a good idea at all! You and *Jeremiah* are going off to a dig up in the north of England once we get there, right? So I'll be left all alone?"

"We'll only be gone two weeks or so. Then we'll all have some time to sightsee before we return home."

"But Cornelia's going with you?"

"Yes. She's actually coming out of retirement to give a paper."

"So it's just going to be Zoe and me the whole time?"

"Oh, there'll be someone there to watch you. Someone who'll do the cooking, that sort of thing. I'm so glad Cornelia decided to go with us. Took some coaxing, I must tell you. She's become almost a recluse since her daughter died."

"Was that Zoe's mother?"

"Yes. Her name was Rachel, and she was Cornelia's only child."

"What happened to her?"

"It was tragic. She died in a helicopter crash."

"Did you know her, too?"

"No, I never did. She and Cornelia were never very close, I'm afraid. Totally different temperaments. Cornelia is a wonderful woman, a brilliant intellect, but she does have a tendency to be a bit strong-willed."

"*Pigheaded* is the word you're looking for, Barbara," my father said, sticking his head in the doorway.

"Hey, she's not that bad. Anyway, I haven't seen Cornelia in years. That's how your father and I met, you know, on one of her digs. But she stopped doing fieldwork ages ago. She was teaching at Oxford when Rachel died. Then, when she took custody of her granddaughter, she retired completely and bought this farm in Olbourne. It's called Rose Farm, and it's supposed to be quite lovely."

How lovely could it be, I wondered, if I was going to be locked up in a house all day listening to Zoe Mitchell playing her flute—or whatever it is that gifted people do that makes them so *gifted.*

But in the end, as always happens no matter how liberated parents think they are, *they* made the decision, so there I was, watching a movie that was really dumb while almost everyone else had settled down in the quiet cabin and was pretending to be asleep. I say *pretending* because I don't believe for one minute that anybody could really go to sleep on an airplane. Either you're excited like I was or you're scared to death, right?

There was a guy I'd been watching since we boarded who I thought was acting awfully suspicious. He was sitting three seats ahead of us on the other side of the aisle, dressed all in black—and he wasn't a priest. When we first got on the plane, he kept jumping out of his seat and looking all around the cabin, as if he were deciding which of us to take as hostages. I mentioned this to my father, but he said he was probably just a nervous flier. Then I watched him make three trips to the bathroom. That's not the kind of thing I usually keep track of, but I figured that's where he probably hid the hand grenades. I glanced around to see if I could pick out his accomplice because they hardly ever do these things alone, but most of the people near us looked like families. There were even babies on board. I was really jealous of them. The one across the way, who slept through the whole trip, was only about two hours old, and here it was taking its first airplane ride. How embarrassing. It was eleven years ahead of me.

Finally, I did sleep a little, but only about a nap's worth. And when we arrived at Heathrow Airport in London, we went through customs right behind my friend the hijacker. I must say he did look a lot more relaxed, even laughing and joking with the man who was checking his luggage. But then I figured that was probably only a ploy to distract the customs official because our guy is not a hijacker at all but a smuggler. I consider myself a good judge of character, and I could tell he wasn't just an ordinary person like you and me.

We had rented a car for the drive to Olbourne, which is the tiny village only a few hours outside of London where Cornelia Jessup lives. In England, I soon discovered, everything is reversed: The driver sits on the right side, and all the traffic goes the opposite from the way it does in the United States. That didn't seem like such a monumental problem until we got our car, loaded it up, and my father pulled out into a lane of oncoming traffic. My mother started screaming, and my father muttered something about just being a little bit sleepy.

My father has been to England lots of times, but he says it always takes him a few days to get back into the swing of things. I looked out the window, hoping to catch a glimpse of Queen Elizabeth or Prince Charles, but there were just ordinary people everywhere.

My father seemed unfazed even as he kept slamming on the brakes and driving the car so close to the left side of the road that the branches of trees were breaking off and falling in the window next to me.

Every few minutes my mother would yell out,

"Watch it! Jeremiah, you're going to get us all killed!"

And my father would sound really hurt. "Barbara, where's your faith? Have I ever gotten us killed? Uh-oh, here's that roundabout I hate . . ."

The shakiness in my father's voice made me brace myself. Up till now, he hadn't seemed aware of the danger, of how really bad he was driving. What was a roundabout, I wondered, and how terrible must it be to jerk my father into reality?

A roundabout turned out to be just a plain old traffic circle, only there were about seven or eight exits out of the circle—seven or eight chances to smash into another car. There seemed to be very strict rules about which car went which way at what time, a pattern that was to be followed if you intended to come out alive.

"Do you know what you're supposed to do, Jeremiah?" my mother said, her voice trembling.

"No, but that's never stopped me before!" my father said heartily, and with that, he clutched the wheel tightly in both hands, yelled, "Hold on!" to my mother and me, and drove straight through the roundabout to the other side, not obeying the traffic signals, not looking to the left or right or seeming to hear the honks and curses of the other drivers.

This was turning out to be more fun than I had thought! For one thing, I was seeing a whole new side of my parents. My mother was sitting in the front seat quivering like a feminist nightmare while my father had suddenly turned into Indiana Jones. (Well, all right, maybe I exaggerate. But he was certainly more *awake* than he normally is.)

Yes, indeed, I thought, as we hurled along the M10 out of London at seventy miles per hour—on the wrong side of the road—if we could just speed right on past the exit marked Olbourne, and right on by the gifted Zoe and her flute . . . well then, you never know.

This trip might not be so bad, after all.

My first glimpse of Rose Farm was of two beautiful golden retrievers leaping wildly at the sight of our car coming around the bend. They were imprisoned behind a huge old wooden fence and were barking almost hysterically, as if they'd been penned in too long and needed a run across the moors to release all their doggie energy. (Either that or some constable had called ahead to warn them that the notorious Jeremiah Gales was still behind the wheel and headed their way.)

"It's beautiful here, isn't it," my father said as we pulled into the driveway.

"Pay attention!" my mother snapped, which had become her automatic answer to anything—even a burp—coming from the driver's seat.

When my father came to a bumpy stop and turned off the engine, the car made a hissing sound, as if all the tension of our two-hour drive was being released slowly, like the gas from a helium balloon.

The door of the house opened and a woman appeared, clapping her hands in the dogs' direction and calling out, "Daisy! Winston! Hush up now!" She squinted in the sudden sunlight, as if the interior of the cottage had been too dark. I'm saying "cottage" because that's the way it was described to me, but it was a good-sized house—in fact, it was two good-sized houses fastened together in the middle, with matching doors and windows. I looked around as I got out of the car and saw nothing but green fields and rock walls and here and there on the landscape old homes that looked as if they'd been built of stone centuries ago. Sheep were grazing peacefully in a nearby field. "Barbara . . . Jeremiah! My, but you made good time. I wasn't expecting you for another hour or so!"

Cornelia Jessup had a lined face with a strong nose, clear blue eyes, and gray hair pulled back severely into a knot at the back of her head. She was much smaller than I had imagined. As she came forward and gave my mother a hug, I was surprised to see that Barbara towered over the older woman. I guess it's possible to be taller than your mentor, but until that moment, I had never considered the possibility.

"Did you have a good trip down? The traffic wasn't too bad, was it? The motorway can be dreadful at this time of year!"

She was holding my mother at arm's length with large, man-sized hands and scrutinizing her as if she were a child.

"It's so good to see you, Cornelia," my mother said.

"I'm sorry Zoe's not here to greet you," she said to me, "but she should be back soon. She always seems to have so much to do! I'm afraid she's just a bit of a gadfly!"

This Princess Diana–like creature began to swim in front of my eyes, and I had to shake my head to clear the vision.

Cornelia Jessup took us on a tour of her house and, just as you'd expect in a place called Rose Farm, there were blossoms everywhere. Not just the real ones, although there were plenty of those, but also ones printed on slipcovers and throw pillows and upstairs on the comforters and curtains.

Then she handed my father the key to the house next door, and we saw that our house was almost exactly like Cornelia's own. On the first floor there was a dining room, a living room (she called it a parlor), a pretty big kitchen, plus a bathroom and a place to do the laundry.

When we went upstairs, they said I could choose my own room. It was an easy decision. The one I picked had a lovely view and was done in what Cornelia called peaches and cream. My parents, of course, got the master bedroom, with its own bath, which meant the bath in the hall was all mine!

"Isn't this lovely," my mother said. "I only wish we were staying here longer!"

"So do I," said Cornelia, "but you may as well make use of it while you're here. These old rooms are empty most of the time. Now, take your time to get settled and then come over and have a visit. I'll put the kettle on and we'll have some lunch," she said, going back downstairs.

I enjoyed unpacking, greeting my clothes like wrinkled old friends I hadn't seen in ages. After being cooped up with fourteen girls in a barracks at Camp Minnehaha, I felt like royalty as I shoved my T-shirts into the drawer and sat bouncing on the double bed, trying it out. Then I went over to the window, taking in the spectacular view. It was almost scary. Where were the other buildings? Why couldn't I see the air like I could in New York? The only sounds were made by a couple of birds in a tree beneath my window. If I concentrated, I could hear the dogs barking at each other . . . but very softly this time, as if they were deep in conversation.

As I stood there taking it all in, a girl on a bicycle came around the bend in the road, the basket on her handlebars full of packages. She slid to a stop at the side of the driveway, kicked the brake, and hurried into the house. It had to be Zoe, and from the safe distance of the bedroom window, she didn't look so fantastic. She was small like her grandmother, so I had the advantage there, and her hair was short, dark, and nondescript. I can handle *her,*

I thought, as I heard my parents in the hallway.

"Are you unpacked, Cory? Let's go down. I really could use a cup of tea."

The two houses were connected by a door that led from our kitchen to their dining room. For some stupid reason, I felt like the Mertzes in those old "I Love Lucy" reruns, where Fred and Ethel are always popping in and out through the kitchen. At our building in New York City, we hardly ever see our neighbors, and we only say "hello" if we happen to be getting our mail at the same time. I can't remember anybody from one of the other apartments ever being in our kitchen. My parents call it respecting one another's privacy. That's very big in New York.

Cornelia welcomed us into the dining room, where the table was set with beautiful china on a fancy lace tablecloth. I hate tea, but the rest of the lunch looked pretty good: There were trays of little sandwiches and wonderful things full of whipped cream, so I immediately got interested. I kept looking around while the grown-ups talked, wondering where Zoe was. Maybe she didn't know that I knew she was home, and she figured she could stay out of the way, probably studying, even though it was summer vacation, and never even have to meet us.

As if she had read my thoughts, Cornelia looked over at me and said, "Zoe has returned, but I'm afraid she has a dreadful headache and she won't be able to join us. Perhaps a bit later you girls will get together. I know she's really longing to meet you."

I'll bet she is, I thought. She didn't look like she had a headache ten minutes ago.

"Well, now, I imagine you'd like to get your bearings a bit. I could take you into the village if you like."

"There's no need for you to bother, Cornelia. We can walk in, can't we? It didn't seem very far."

"It isn't, only a mile or so down the road."

"Why don't we drive in?" my father asked.

"Oh, no, Jeremiah, you shouldn't do any more driving," my mother said, a bit too quickly. "You must be exhausted."

"Not at all. I feel invigorated. A challenge always does that to me."

"Even so, I think we could all use some exercise after being cooped up on the plane. Right, Cory?"

"Right!" I felt bad that I almost shouted my agreement because my father looked disappointed. I think he fancied himself rather dashing behind the wheel and was about to get himself a helmet and some snazzy racing gloves.

Later in the afternoon, we did walk into town, and it didn't seem far at all. It was very quiet and peaceful. Every now and then we'd stop to admire an old cottage with its garden spilling blossoms from the front door out into the road. Every now and then we'd also leap into the bushes as a car came roaring up behind us—we were walking on the wrong side of the road, of course.

Coming into the village, we followed the narrow street that bent to the right and looked for the grocery store where Cornelia said we could buy some things and have them delivered to the house.

When we found it, the aisles in the tiny shop were so narrow that there was hardly room for the three of us, and all the brands were so different I couldn't even tell what some of the things were. Barbara and Jeremiah stood debating the merits of every item they pulled from the shelf. My father had taken out his glasses and was examining each label as if it were a rare artifact pulled from the tomb of King Tut. After I had trailed them aimlessly for awhile, feeling large and ungainly because I kept getting in the way of little old ladies who were carrying string bags for their daily supply of groceries, I said, "I'm going to look around outside, okay?"

I had seen some kids about my own age down the street, so I left the shop and crossed over, hoping I'd catch up with them. I passed a "chemist," which I knew was a drugstore, but when I got to the corner, the kids I'd seen had vanished. But a boy and a girl were standing together leafing through some magazines at a newsstand. I strolled over casually and began to scan the racks.

No *Seventeen.* No *American Girl.* I thumbed through

something called *Queen.* Very sophisticated, like our *Harper's Bazaar* or *Vogue.* (Probably Zoe has a subscription.) While I pretended to look at the magazines, I couldn't help eavesdropping on the conversation next to me.

" 'Tis not."

" 'Tis *so.*"

"You're a liar, Owen Parks!"

"Who you callin' a liar? You're the biggest liar there is. You're the biggest liar in the whole of Olbourne. You're the biggest liar in the whole British Empire . . . in the whole *universe,* maybe."

"I hate you."

"So who cares?"

"You'll care soon enough if I tell *Mum.*"

"Go ahead. Just see if I care."

I glanced over and noted the same fiery red hair and freckles and the same flat, knobby nose. They *had* to be brother and sister.

The girl threw down the magazine and, folding her arms defiantly, turned her back on her brother as if this was the ultimate punishment. It must be very frustrating having a brother like that, I thought. Nothing you said or did or threatened could get to him. I picked up the magazine she'd been reading. It was called *British Teen,* and while it wasn't as good as what we have back home, it was probably the best I was going to get. I checked the price and, fishing in my pocket, pulled out a bunch of coins and stood staring at them dumbly. I was about to go up and thrust my hand out to the store clerk, trusting in his honesty, when the boy called Owen Parks unexpectedly spoke.

"Can I help you?"

I looked up, and he seemed to have become a different boy. Now that his sister wasn't bothering him, the air of toughness had disappeared, as if he were a boxer who's gone to his corner and taken off his gloves to relax until the next round.

"I'm not sure of the money yet." (I didn't honestly think I'd *ever* be sure of the money, but I couldn't admit that to him.)

He took three copper coins out of my hand and went over and handed them to the clerk, who said, "Thank you." Then he came back and stood looking at me as I shoved the rest of the money in my pocket.

"You from America?" he said.

"Yes. How did you know?"

He laughed, but it was a nice laugh, not like he was making fun of me.

"Your accent," he said.

Accent? What accent? *I* don't have any accent; *you* have an accent!

"Oh."

"You staying here in Olbourne?"

"Yes, at Rose Farm. Do you know it?"

The friendly look vanished.

"Aye, I know where it is. Are you a friend of Miz Jessup's then? Or her granddaughter?"

"Actually, neither. I mean, my parents are friends of Mrs. Jessup, but I haven't even met her granddaughter yet."

His sister had slowly turned around as we talked, and I knew she was listening to us. Now she spoke up. "You really from America?" she asked. Curiosity had obviously won out over her fight with Owen.

"Uh-huh. New York."

"Omigosh, that's even better."

"What d' you mean?"

"Well, I've never really known anybody from the States, I mean someone my age, and New York ... it's fair exciting."

I began to feel great. This was fun. This was almost like being a celebrity. "Yeah, well, New York *is* pretty exciting," I said.

"You must be awfully brave to actually live there. You *do* mean you really live there all the time—you don't just visit once in a while on holiday?"

"Of course I really live there! But I'm not brave. Why should I be?"

"Why, with all the murders and such. I think I'd need to carry a gun or something. Is that what you do?"

"No. Where'd you hear that?"

"Oh, I hear things. And everybody knows about New York. We see it on the telly."

"Well, it's not like that where I live. I mean, there are good neighborhoods and bad neighborhoods, just like in London."

"I don't think I could live in London, either," she said, shaking her head solemnly.

"Oh" was all I managed to say in answer to that. There was a pause then, and I realized I should be getting back to my folks. But instead, I asked, "So, do you guys know Mrs. Jessup's granddaughter?"

His sister giggled, but Owen just stared at me for a moment. Finally he answered. "You mean Zoe Mitchell? *Hardly,*" he said.

"How come?"

"What do you mean, *how come?*"

"I mean, it's such a small place, and you kids are all about the same age. Aren't you in the same class or something?"

"You may be from New York sure enough, but you certainly don't know very much, do you!"

"Why—what do you mean?" I said, wanting to back away from him now because he'd become so unfriendly.

"Zoe Mitchell thinks she's too good for the likes of us. She has a tutor," his sister volunteered.

"Oh," I said. Then I added, "I guess that's because she's so gifted." What else could I say? They seemed so mad about everything all of a sudden!

Owen tugged at his sister's sleeve. "Come on, Patsy, stop your gossiping or we'll be late."

"We've got to go now. See you anon."

I wanted to say something else so they wouldn't go away mad, but before I could protest, the two of them took off and disappeared down the hill and through the archway into the center of the village.

Where did they live? I wondered. There didn't seem to be any houses down that way, just some shops. And of course, there was the crumbling old Lion's Head Inne & Publick House that sat on the square.

But nobody could live there—or could they?

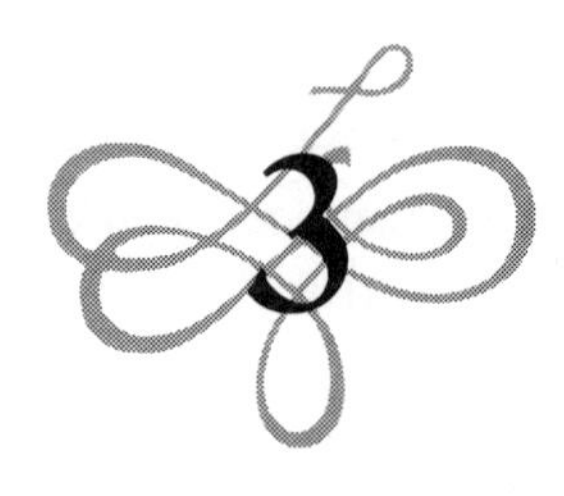

"I wonder where Cornelia's granddaughter is keeping herself?" my mother said, as we sat in the dining room the next evening finishing dinner. "I wouldn't have insisted on you coming if I hadn't thought there'd be someone here your own age for company."

"But I don't mind, really I don't."

"Well, I certainly hope she makes an appearance before we leave in the morning. I think it would be really rude if she didn't."

"Don't worry, Barbara. If the child is as intellectually gifted as Cornelia has suggested, she's bound to be a bit of a loner. I'm sure she and Cory will hit it off once they get together."

"You're probably right. But I do hope that this Bridget is dependable."

"Who is Bridget? Is she the lady who's staying with us?"

"Right. I thought I told you. She's one of the villagers. I believe she works down at the inn, but she's agreed to stay here and take care of things while we're gone."

"Great."

"This meal isn't bad, is it?" my mother said, passing the platter in my direction.

"Hmmm . . ." was all I trusted myself to say as I turned down a second helping.

I would never have admitted it to my mother, but I hadn't been looking forward to her trying to cook in an English kitchen with a foreign stove. Last night we'd all had jet lag and had just made some sandwiches, but tonight my worst fears had come true: My mother had managed to turn out a chicken dish that tasted as if the bird had been soaking for days in Ivory Liquid.

As we started to clear the dishes, a knock came on the kitchen door, and when my mother opened it, Cornelia Jessup was standing there, her hands folded in front of her as if she were praying.

"I hope I'm not interrupting your dinner?"

"Oh, no, Cornelia, we've just finished. Please come in."

"No, no. I just thought perhaps you could come through and have tea, or coffee if you prefer, and take another look at the schedule. I've got some more notes, and it will make it less hectic for us in the morning."

"Certainly, Cornelia. We have our coffee right here; we'll just bring it on through. Cory, you want to join us?"

I stood there debating what to do and then, as if maybe my mere presence in the house would shame Zoe, I stepped through and followed the grown-ups into the parlor.

As I settled on the flowery couch, wanting very much to tuck my sneakers up under me but deciding against it, I became aware of a creaking noise in the ceiling over my head. It was a very old house, just like the one we were living in, and you could hear movement easily from one room to another. Obviously, someone was walking up there, and you didn't have to be a genius to know who it was. I looked over at my parents, who were deep in conversation with Cornelia, and wondered if they heard it, too. I was going to say something but decided not to and instead spent a few moments looking around the room. There were photographs everywhere. Some were small and clustered in bunches on tabletops; others were larger and hung in groups or singly on the walls. Most of them were old, and some looked interesting; and since no one was paying any attention to me, I decided to investigate.

I walked around the room slowly, the way my parents do when we're in a museum. There were pictures of Cornelia Jessup when she was very young, standing outside a pyramid in Egypt; one of her standing next to a huge open pit in a strange-looking forest; and one of her onboard a ship with a group of people who looked like they might be other archaeologists. There was even a picture of her receiving an award from Queen Elizabeth!

On a lace-covered tabletop, I saw more pictures, but these were family ones: Cornelia holding an infant, Cornelia with a little girl on her lap, pictures of the young girl growing up. In all the later pictures, the girl looked like Cornelia Jessup, only in different, more modern clothes, and she seemed always to be somewhere foreign doing something adventurous, just like Cornelia. If this was Zoe's mother, boy, did the genes get mixed up. Or maybe Zoe just inherited the scholarly part and none of the adventure. Then I noticed that there was something else in these photographs that was missing from the ones of Cornelia. Her daughter was always pictured with a camera slung over her shoulder. In some of them, she was behind a mounted tripod, and somebody was taking a shot of her taking a shot.

"Was your daughter a photographer?" I asked.

Cornelia Jessup looked up at me over her glasses. "Yes, she was," she said quietly. There was a pause, as if she wanted to make sure I wasn't going to interrupt them with any more stupid questions, and then she went back to their conversation.

I realized then that maybe I shouldn't have mentioned her daughter. It was very sad that she had died, but from what I knew, she was a bit of an eccentric—that's the word my mother had used—and I guess she and Cornelia had been as opposite as two people can be.

I slipped out of the room unnoticed and wandered down the hall, looking at all the photographs lining the walls. I was getting bored with the pictures of Cornelia Jessup and found myself more intrigued with the pictures of her daughter, Rachel. At least she seemed to be having fun in the pictures, and when I came to one of her with her arm around a little girl, I knew it had to be Zoe. The same Zoe who at this very moment was thumping around noisily overhead.

The light in the hallway was dim, and I had to strain to make out some of the pictures. One showed the little girl, now a bit older and very clearly the Zoe I had seen in the driveway, brandishing a camera with a big smile on her face. The next one was of Zoe, too, but I couldn't make it out because by now I was just as far away from the light as I could possibly be. So I did a simple thing: I took the picture off the wall and walked down to the end of the hallway where there was a table with a lamp and I could get a better look.

It was Zoe all right, posing in the entrance to the Lion's Head Inne. As I started to walk back with the picture, holding it casually by its side, something slipped out of the frame and fell to the floor. For a moment I stood examining the slit in the back of the picture, thinking what a neat idea and what a great hiding place it was. Then I reached down and picked up what had been hidden there. It was a second photograph, and I glanced at it quickly. Then, seeing what it was, I brought it back to the table where I could examine it more closely.

It was another picture of Zoe, almost exactly like the one in the frame, only now there were two older men in the picture with her. Both the men had beards and were dressed in old-fashioned clothes. As I compared the two photos, I noticed that in both pictures Zoe looked exactly the same, as if they were taken the same day. She was wearing the identical white shorts and striped T-shirt, and she had the same smile on her face. But if I hadn't known it was Zoe, I would have sworn it was her grandmother or even her great-grandmother because the picture had the grainy, yellowed, old-fashioned look of a picture taken a very long time ago.

"Put that back!"

I whirled around and stood staring up at the famous Zoe Mitchell, who had appeared at the top of the staircase like some sort of demon. While I stood there, too surprised to speak, she hurried down the stairs, snatched the picture out of my hands, and—after reinserting the photo—hung it back in its proper place.

"Sor-ry!" I said, with all the sarcasm I could muster.

She just glowered at me for a moment, saying nothing but letting me get a good look at her. Her heavy, dark brows were knitted together, forming a canopy over the pug nose, thick lips, and pouty expression that made up the rest of her face.

"You shouldn't touch things that aren't yours. You Americans are so incredibly rude."

"Rude? What do you call somebody who sneaks around and pretends she has a headache just so she doesn't have to say hello? Well, don't worry; I won't bother you anymore. We'll be back in the States before you know it." I turned, hoping my parents hadn't heard my outburst and planning to sneak back into our house, but she stopped me, pulling at my arm.

"Wait; don't go. I'm sorry." I stared at her. "Why were you looking at that picture? Do you know who's in it?"

"It's *you.*"

"I know it's me. I mean, the others. Do you know who they are?" There was a strange urgency in her voice.

"No, of course not. Don't you?" She looked down at her sensible, laced-up shoes and shook her head. "But they're in the picture with you."

"Not really," she said quietly. Then, as we heard

the others get up and start to leave the living room, she bolted upstairs, whispering, "Please don't tell!"

My mother and father came into the other end of the hallway, followed by Cornelia. My mother was still holding her coffee cup.

"Did we hear you talking to someone, Cory?" she asked.

I didn't know what to say. Zoe had pleaded, "Don't tell!" But don't tell what? That I had taken the picture off the wall? That she had come down the stairs and put it back? Or even just that I had seen it—or that I had seen her? It was too exhausting.

"I was just mumbling to myself," I fibbed.

"You *must* be tired!" Jeremiah said, laughing. "Come on, we've got to get on the road early in the morning."

When we said good-night to Cornelia Jessup, I could have sworn she gave me a strange look.

I went to bed early and read awhile, then turned off my light and tried to get to sleep. But sleep wouldn't come. I kept thinking of Zoe and the weird picture that was hidden in back of the regular one. I thought of how maybe she was sleeping right across the wall from me, and I tried to remember what she had said before we were interrupted. I had pointed out that the men she claimed not to know were right there in the picture with her. I remembered it just as I drifted off to sleep.

What she had said was "Not *really.*"

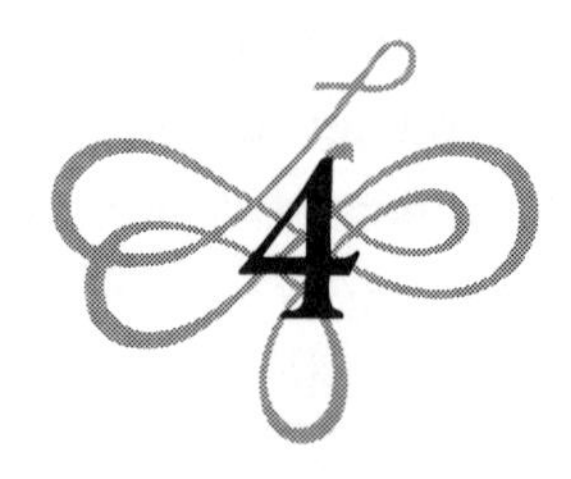

I stood frozen by our kitchen door, only half awake, barefoot and still in my pajamas. I knew I shouldn't eavesdrop, but I couldn't move.

The voice that did most of the talking, the stronger voice, was Cornelia's. I could only guess that the other person was Zoe, and I missed half of what she said because she kept sniffling and blowing her nose. If it had been anybody but the perfect Zoe Mitchell, I would have thought she was crying.

"You cannot hide in your room the whole time she's here. I'll not have it."

That was the first thing I made out and, as you can imagine, it really caught my interest.

"I'm not going to hide ... just ... my headache ..."

"You and your headaches. You know what Dr.

Marsh said about your headaches. You must meet the Gales and be properly introduced."

There was more mumbling from Zoe, with great honking in a handkerchief—it must have been a wingding of a cold—and then I heard a door closing. The soft clanking of dishes being cleared from the dining room table was followed by an almost scary silence.

I had shuffled downstairs to say good-bye to my folks and have some breakfast. I certainly hadn't intended to listen in on any conversations. I mean, I have better things to do. (All right, so maybe I don't . . . yet.) But something about Cornelia Jessup's voice caught my attention. Even muffled behind the kitchen door, there was an almost hysterical quality to it, as if she was really upset about something.

I waited a moment and then silently I put the milk back in our refrigerator and sat down to finish the last of my scrambled eggs. My parents had eaten their breakfast and were almost ready to leave. I was beginning to think that Bridget wasn't going to show and I'd be stuck all alone here with sniffling Zoe, when someone knocked on the front door.

It was Cornelia, with a woman she introduced as Bridget Collins. Bridget wasn't as old as Cornelia. She was more my mother's age, and she was wiry and thin, like maybe she was a runner, with sandy hair and freckles. After introductions were over, we all stood around in our living room without speaking for a few seconds. Then Bridget broke the silence.

"Where's Zoe—not still sleeping?" she asked Cornelia.

"Uh, yes, I'm afraid she is." *Liar!*

"That girl is going to sleep her life away!" she said.

"Oh, I'm sure she'll be in very shortly to meet Cory."

Bridget made a face. "You mean you two haven't met yet?"

There was a pause, and then my mother said, "Well, we just got here the other day ..."

"Oh, but we'll have to do something about that, won't we?" Bridget said, and she turned and marched—that's really what it looked like—through to the other house. Bridget seemed like a real take-charge kind of person, and I liked her right away. For a few minutes we stood there awkwardly, Cornelia reminding my father to stop for "petrol" and my mother checking and rechecking her bag to make sure she had everything.

Then Bridget returned with Zoe Mitchell walking two steps behind her. (Was I the only one to notice that Zoe Mitchell obviously slept *fully dressed?*)

"Zoe, this is Mr. and Mrs. Gales and their daughter, Cory."

"How do you do, Zoe. We're so glad to meet you."

"Your grandmother has told us so much about you."

"We've met," I said.

Zoe looked so startled when I said it that I knew I'd made a big mistake. Obviously, she didn't want anyone to know about the meeting in the hallway. "Uh, I mean, I saw you in the driveway when we first got here."

"Oh. Nice to meet you," she said then, to all of us.

There's a boy in our class they call Shy Joey because you practically have to pry words out of him with a crowbar, and Zoe had the same look about her. But maybe with her it wasn't shyness. What was it Patsy had said: "Zoe Mitchell thinks she's too good for the likes of us." But at least she didn't look as scary as she had last night on the staircase.

"Now you girls be good for Bridget!" Cornelia said brightly. She seemed relieved that we'd finally been introduced.

After we'd said our good-byes and the car had pulled out of the driveway, Zoe whirled around suddenly and faced Bridget with the demon face I'd seen the night before.

"You had no right to drag me in here like that!"

"Oh, go on with you. You'll behave for me or I'll take a stick to you and that's the truth!"

Bridget was grinning as she said it, and she gave Zoe's rear end a playful swipe as Zoe flounced out of the room.

Scratch that bit about Shy Joey.

"What is her *problem?*" I asked.

"Never you mind; I can handle Zoe. Now, are you going to move into the house with Zoe and me?"

Did I have a choice?

"I kind of like it where I am. Could I just stay here?"

"Of course you can. It's really all one big house, anyway. They just sliced up these manor houses years ago, 'cause no one could keep them up, and that's a fact! Why don't you get your clothes on while I find out what her ladyship is up to. Then we can make some plans for the day."

I got dressed and returned in jiffy time, but I could tell by Bridget's face as she sat in the living room that there were no "plans for the day."

"I'm sorry. I tried my best, but Zoe's gotten one of her headaches."

"That's okay; she doesn't look like much fun anyway."

I guess it wasn't the most polite thing to say, but I was tired of being the polite one.

"Don't be too harsh on her, Cory. I think maybe you're right; Zoe has got problems."

"Or maybe she's just a brat," I said.

"Oh, no. You've got to remember, Cory, the poor child lost her mother in that terrible accident, I don't think she ever knew her father, and then she comes here to stay with the grandmother and, well now, I mean no disrespect, but Mrs. Jessup is what my mum calls a person of measured merriment."

"Measured merri . . . I get it. It means she's a grouch, right?"

"Well, now, I'll deny I ever said anything if you go and quote me on that!" she said, laughing.

"Oh, I won't," I said. "But why doesn't Zoe go out and play with the other kids? What does she do all day?"

"I don't really know. She seems frightened a good deal of the time, poor thing, but what she's got to be afraid of in a wee village like Olbourne, I can't fathom. I can see it if she was off on one of those jaunts she used to take with her mother. God rest her soul, she took that child to some weird places. Aye, I'm afraid she misses her mum something fierce, but she won't admit it. She seems to be most contented when she's able to sneak off by herself with that camera. It was her mother's, you know. Her mum was a big-shot photographer."

"I heard."

I felt a little bit guilty then. It must be horrible to lose your mom. And to have no father . . . and, on top of it all, to have Cornelia Jessup be your grandmother! A shudder went through me. I wanted to tell Bridget that I didn't think Zoe seemed frightened, but then I remembered last night when I found that picture. She sure seemed scared then.

"At any rate, we just have to try to be kind, all right?"

She's the hostess from hell, and you're asking me to be *kind?*

"Of course," I said.

"Tell you what. You entertain yourself today, and tonight we'll all go into town for the weekly band concert. I think you'll really enjoy that."

"Wonderful," I said, smiling this really phony smile I almost never use outside of the classroom.

How Bridget talked Zoe into going to the band concert I don't know, but by seven o'clock the three of us were on our way, and when we reached the village square, I was surprised to see the crowds that were there already. I'd had no idea that there were so many people living in Olbourne! It seemed to be such a tiny place but, like those circus acts where all the clowns pile out of one little car, the band concert had acted as a magnet, drawing the villagers out of their homes from miles around. Some of them stood around the fountain, where members of the band had gathered in their bright red uniforms, but lots of them were spilling over onto the lawns and fields nearby. There were old people sitting in folding chairs and little kids running around in circles. The band was warming up by making strange sounds on their instruments: bleeps, honks, toots, clangs, and even a few ear-shattering drum rolls.

Zoe Mitchell hadn't said anything all the way into town, so now, after we spread a blanket on the grass and Bridget went over to talk to a neighbor, I decided maybe I should try, as Bridget put it, to be "kind."

"I'm glad you decided to come," I said. But all she did was shrug her shoulders, so we just sat there in silence for a moment. After a while, I thought about how this was the first time I'd had a chance to ask her about that picture, so I said, "Last night, why did you say what you did about that picture?"

"What?"

"You said the men weren't really in the picture with you. But of course they were. So why'd you say that?"

"Please don't talk about that picture."

"Why not?"

"Just because. *Please.*"

I realized then that she had tears in her eyes, and I knew that Bridget was right. She might be a brat some of the time, but right now it was obvious Zoe Mitchell was scared silly, and it had something to do with that photograph.

"Listen, I haven't told anyone about the picture. And I never will if that's what you want. But I just want to say, if you *do* want to talk about it, whatever it is, I don't mind. I mean, I'm going to be here for awhile, and we're staying in the same house practically . . ."

She looked at me with a puzzled expression, as if she couldn't understand what I was saying, almost as if I were speaking a foreign language. And suddenly a really wild idea hit me: Zoe Mitchell didn't have any friends. Probably had never had any. I mean, really, truly, there wasn't anyone she could talk to about things the way I could talk to Diane. And I thought how that must be the most awful thing in the world. No wonder she looked so sad!

But she didn't answer me, and so neither of us spoke for awhile, and even though there was noise all around us, it seemed totally still and eerie. After the band started up, we sat listening to the music for a few minutes as they played "Up, Up and Away," "Raindrops Keep Falling on My Head," and something else I couldn't identify.

Bridget had returned and settled down on the blanket with us, and all of a sudden she gave a shout.

"Hey, Owen, what're you doin' with yourself?"

I looked to where she was pointing and recognized the redheaded boy from the other day. His sister and another boy were with him.

"Hi there, Bridget," he called back as the three of them came toward us.

"Owen, have you met Cory Gales?"

"Aye, the other day."

"She the American?" the other boy said to him, as if I weren't even there. When Owen nodded, the boy looked back at me and sniggered.

"This here's Gerald McCray," Owen said.

"And I'm Patsy," Owen's sister said, smiling.

"Hi," I said.

"And you all know Zoe, of course," Bridget said. There was silence while everybody sort of nodded and Zoe examined the stitching on the red-and-blue blanket we were sitting on. "So, Owen, how's your mum getting on without me?" Bridget went on.

"I reckon she misses you," he said. "We have to help out sometimes. In fact, we should be over there now. We have to give her a hand as soon as the concert's over."

"You guys have to work?" Gerald said.

"Not till the end. Come and wait with us on the steps. Our mum'll call us when she needs us."

"So long, Bridget," they called as they started to leave.

"You kids should go with them," Bridget said, nodding to Zoe and me.

"You want to come? You can see the band better from the inn," Patsy said.

I jumped up and started to follow them, glad to be included. Then I stopped, realizing that Zoe hadn't moved.

"Come on, Zoe, let's go over and stand on the steps."

She looked up at me with eyes that were suddenly wild and frantic. Then she began to shake her head violently.

"No, I won't go there. I don't want to!"

"Why not?" I asked, and was sorry right away that I'd pushed it. The look on her face was trying to tell me why not.

"Ah, don't force her if she doesn't want to come!" Owen said, then to me, "You coming or not?"

I glanced at Bridget, and she motioned to me to go on ahead.

"What'd I tell you?" Patsy said, as we made our way to the bandstand. "She thinks she's too good for the likes of us."

Before I could answer her, an old woman walked by and called out, "Hello, children. Enjoying the music, are you?"

"Yes, ma'am," Patsy said politely, as the woman continued on her way through the crowd.

"Did you hear," Owen said, "she hasn't got a picture of Rascal yet, and he's her favorite."

"No picture of Rascal? Why not?"

"I guess no visitors have come by with a camera."

"What're you guys talking about?" I asked. By this time, we were standing so near the band, I had to shout to be heard over the music.

"That was Mrs. Mulcahey," Gerald said, giggling. "She owns the other big farm in Olbourne. But it's not roses she grows!"

"What is it, then?" I asked.

"Pigs!" Patsy said, squealing like one herself.

"Oh. So what's so funny about pigs?"

"Nothing," she said, "only Mrs. Mulcahey thinks they're her children. She talks to them; she has names for all of them; she even has pictures of them. You'd understand if you saw her gift shop. We could go by sometime, if you like."

"Sure," I said. Great! I didn't have to depend on Bridget forcing Zoe to be my friend.

"Patsy, do you still have your dad's camera to use?" Gerald asked.

"Naw. He won't let me have it since I dropped it that time."

"You got one?" Gerald asked me.

I shook my head. "My folks do, but they took it with them."

"Drats."

"But I know who has one."

"Who?"

"Zoe Mitchell. Maybe she'll let me borrow it." Was I out of my mind?

"We were planning to pay Mrs. Mulcahey a visit tomorrow. You think you could get it by then?"

"You can come with us if you do," Patsy added.

My social life had now reached the point where I was being bribed with an invitation to a pig farm. I couldn't wait till Diane found out. She'd be so jealous!

"I think so," I said, trying to sound humble and grateful at the same time.

"Well, if you get it, meet us in the square about ten o'clock," Owen said, almost as if it was an order.

"Right," I said, as the concert finished with an

earsplitting blast of trumpet and everybody clapped and cheered.

"We've got to get inside," Owen said and, with a wave, he and his sister disappeared into the pub. So they did live there!

"See you anon," Gerald said.

"Right," I said. "I gotta go, too."

I hurried back, but when I got to the blanket, Bridget was alone.

"What happened to Zoe?" I asked, feeling guilty and not knowing why.

"She went home. One of her headaches," Bridget said, raising her eyebrows as she folded the blanket.

As we headed back to Rose Farm, the awful truth slowly dawned on me. I must have been so psyched to have them include me in their plans that I'd temporarily taken leave of my senses. What possessed me to think that Zoe Mitchell would be willing to share her precious camera with me, when so far she didn't seem too keen on our even sharing the same planet?

"Why do you think she wouldn't come with us?" I asked Bridget.

"I'm sure I have no idea. But don't you worry about it, Cory," she said, giving me a smile as if to reassure me that it wasn't my fault.

Even though I knew she was right, I couldn't get the look on Zoe's face out of my mind. Was I the only one to notice that at the thought of going near the inn, Zoe Mitchell became absolutely terrified?

"It's for a really good cause," I said, as I saw the look of skepticism creep over Bridget's face.

"But Zoe's very protective of her camera, Cory. It was her mother's, you know. Well ... let me see what I can do."

Ever since I'd left the concert last night, I'd been trying to figure out how I could ask Zoe for the camera. I'd decided to try going through Bridget.

It was already nine-thirty and, camera or no camera, I was getting out of this place without waiting around for another "headache" announcement.

To my surprise, when Bridget returned, Zoe was at her side, a camera dangling from a strap around her neck. It was a really big camera, the kind professionals use. Then I realized it was the same one that she had been holding in the photograph.

"You wanted me to come with you and take a picture?" she asked.

"Oh, that's all right; you don't have to come with me. If I could just borrow—"

Before I even finished the sentence, I could see the steel come into her eyes and her lips disappear into a thin, straight line. What was I thinking of! Of course she would never let anyone borrow her camera. In her strange, secret world, lending wasn't allowed.

"I'd have to take the picture," she said. "Nobody else can use the camera."

"Oh, well, then, fine."

She marched over to the door, opened it, and waited for me as if I were the slow kid in class. She is so weird, I thought; why did I have to volunteer the camera? But then, I reminded myself, Zoe was the only reason I was invited out today!

We walked into the village in silence. I mean, in total silence. A couple of times I made comments about things, but all she did was grunt or nod, and I finally gave up.

When we reached the square, Owen and Patsy were waiting by the fountain, and a moment later, Gerald pedaled up on his bicycle. Nobody seemed really interested in talking; the only important thing was that I'd brought a camera and someone to use it.

We started up the hill and out of the village, with the three of them walking in front and Zoe and me tagging along behind. When we reached the fork in the road, we went off down a narrow lane to where a gnarled old tree cast its huge shadow over the road. A white board hung from one of its lower branches.

"This is Mrs. Mulcahey's place," Owen said.

A moment later, Gerald lifted the metal latch on a big wooden gate just like the one that kept the dogs back at Rose Farm, and we went inside. After closing the gate, we walked down a long, dusty road toward the buildings in the distance. As we grew closer, the others walked farther and farther from Zoe and me. They were chattering away, throwing stones to see who could throw the farthest, and didn't even seem to remember that we'd come along.

"There's Mrs. Mulcahey!" Patsy cried, pointing out to the field, where a lone figure was walking toward us. "She's probably got Rascal with her."

As we came closer to the buildings, I could hear and see—as well as smell—Mrs. Mulcahey's "children." There were troughs in rows on either side of the main house, which had roses at the door and curtains in the windows. Then over to the right I saw a sign with an arrow that said GIFT SHOP IN REAR.

We followed the others around the building, and there it was. The gift shop was so tiny that the five of us could barely fit into it, but the girl who was behind the counter reading a magazine barely looked up when we came in. I would have imagined that five customers in this place would have been cause for a celebration, but I guess things were different in Olbourne.

It didn't take me long to discover that this was no ordinary gift shop—this was one with a theme. There were dishcloths and tablecloths, and towels and potholders and ashtrays and key rings—all with pictures of pigs on them. Cute little baby pigs and big, burly sows; some white as snow, some beige, some mud brown. On closer inspection, I could tell that these were real, individual pigs memorialized on all this stuff. "Pearlie" was the centerpiece of a blue-and-white-checked potholder, while a plastic placemat had "Sir Galahad" showing off his entire family.

"Hi, Elizabeth. How's Devon doing with the car?" Owen asked.

"Pretty good. He's got it running fair splendid most of the time."

The little bell over the door tinkled, and Mrs. Mulcahey entered the shop. Her lined, weathered face had a kind expression as she took us all in and said, "Isn't it nice of you children to pay us a visit." Then her clear blue eyes rested on Zoe and me. "And who would these young ladies be?"

"This is Cory," Patsy said quickly. "She's from America—from *New York*." Out of the corner of my eye, I saw Elizabeth put down the magazine and stare at me.

"Well now, you're a long way from home! Would you be staying here in Olbourne?"

Before I could answer, Patsy chimed in again. "At Rose Farm, with Mrs. Jessup and her granddaughter. And this," she said, with a grand sweep of her arm, "is Mrs. Jessup's granddaughter."

"Aye, sure enough," Mrs. Mulcahey said, and her eyes narrowed a bit as if she could go on but decided against it.

"You have lovely gifts here," I said.

"Do you like them? That says something coming from an *American,*" she said, obviously pleased.

"But how do you do it? How do you get the pictures?" I asked.

"Oh, tourists mainly. They give me copies of the pictures they take, and I send them away to London to have them done," she said proudly. Then she added wistfully, "But I don't have one of Rascal."

"That's why we're here," Gerald chirped up. "We're going to take his picture."

Out of the corner of my eye I could see Zoe's hand move protectively around the camera, as if just talking about it was a threat to its security.

"Ach, that's very kind of you children, but I don't think that's possible."

"No sign of him, Grandmother?" Elizabeth asked, with real concern in her voice.

"No, none at all. I can't understand it."

"What's the matter?" Owen asked.

"Rascal's missing again, and I fear this time he's gone for good."

"You mustn't say that!" Elizabeth cried.

"How long's he been gone?" Gerald asked.

"Since yesterday morn."

"Aye, that's a long time for a piglet to get by on its own."

"Are you sure you've searched everywhere?" Owen said, ready, I could tell, to take command of the situation.

"Everywhere I could think of. That's where I was just now, going over the grounds once more. Trouble is, I'm slowing down, and my eyes aren't as good as they used to be. I could have missed him, the wee devil."

"We'll find him!" It was Patsy, not Owen, who was suddenly in charge.

"I don't expect you children to bother yourselves. It's our loss."

"Oh, no, Mrs. Mulcahey, we don't mind. We're good at exploring, and we can form a search party, can't we, gang?" Gerald said eagerly. I wasn't sure if Zoe and I were really included when he spoke about "we," but I nodded with the others anyway.

"Tell us where he was last seen," Owen asked, sounding like Sherlock Holmes as he led us single file out of the shop.

I was last in line, but Zoe had waited for me right outside, even though the others had already started up the hill. As we trudged up after them, I said, "I guess maybe we won't need the camera after all. Sorry you had to waste your time."

She was staring down at her feet while she walked and didn't even glance at me when she spoke.

"Oh, no," she said quietly. "We'll need it."

I shot her a look when she said that, but I didn't have time to ask her what she meant because we had caught up with the others by then, and I was a little out of breath.

"So what's the plan?" I asked Owen.

"We spread out, each of us going in a different direction from the old well."

"Where's that?"

"Over yonder. See the pile of stones under the clump of yew trees?"

I strained my eyes, but I wasn't sure what he meant, and I shook my head.

"I'll show her," Zoe said.

"Okay," he said, glancing at her with a look of surprise, almost as if he had forgotten she was there. I think it was the first word she'd spoken to them since we'd left the village. "Then we go straight until we hit the outer boundaries of the farm, the stone walls, see them?" I peered in the distance and nodded. "Then we head back."

We trudged the rest of the way up the hill to what they called the well, but what looked to me like a pile of rocks around a hole. "Hasn't been used in years. Dry as a bone," Owen informed us when I asked about it. He then pointed out the four directions we were to go in, looking under rocks, in bushes, anywhere a small piglet could have crawled and gotten stuck.

As we began to separate and the others started out across the field, Zoe pulled me back. "Don't go," she said.

"What d'you mean?"

"Don't go," she repeated.

"We have to go; we have to look for the pig. We said we'd try and find him. Look, if you don't want to bother, you wait here."

"No!"

She said it so forcefully, I stopped.

"What's the matter with you?"

"He's not out there," she said.

"Oh, really? You see him around here?" I looked around quickly as if I really expected to see him sitting at my feet.

"Yes, I do," she said.

Now I looked around in earnest. I shielded my eyes from the sun with my hand and looked as hard as I could, as far as I could. I could see the others with their backs to us as they got farther and farther away. I could hear them calling, "Here, Rascal, here, boy. Where are you?"

But there wasn't a piglet in sight.

"Okay, I give up. You're telling me you can see him?"

"Yes, I can," she said, her voice so low now that I could hardly make out what she was saying.

"You want to tell me where?"

"He's right here."

"No, he's not!" I yelled, getting exasperated and a little scared all at the same time. The others had almost reached the wall by now.

"He's in the well. He's still all right, but we'd better hurry."

"He's in the— How do you know?"

"I just do."

I listened, but I couldn't hear a sound. Then I strained over the side to see, but there was only an inky blackness, and the smell of damp and mildew made me jump back.

"How—?" I didn't finish what I was going to say because the others had reached the wall and were on their way back by now, so I just stood there like a dummy.

"Hey, you guys, you didn't even look!" Patsy called out as they got within yelling distance.

"I can't understand it," Owen said, joining us and sitting on the edge of the well. "Where could he be?"

"Be careful," I said, as Patsy sat down next to her brother, tipping back dangerously.

"It's not a long drop. Weeds and brush and leaves filled it up long ago," Owen said.

"Maybe Rascal fell in the well," Zoe said quietly, as if it were something that had just occurred to her.

"Don't be daft," Gerald said.

"He'd not be down there," Owen said firmly.

"Why not?" I listened, hoping and praying I would hear a squeal, but there was only the sound of a breeze rushing through the trees. "Didn't you hear something? I think I did."

Zoe was looking at me warily, as if I were the one who'd gone "daft."

"I don't hear anything," Gerald said.

"Me neither," chimed in Patsy.

"Well, couldn't we get a flashlight and just look? It can't hurt."

"You're daft," Gerald said again.

"Stop saying that, Gerald McCray! You guys haven't come up with a better idea, I notice!"

Suddenly I was frantic to look in the well. Somehow I believed Rascal was down there, just as if I'd seen him myself.

They hesitated, and then Owen said, "Let's humor her, and then we'll have another go round. Patsy, go ask Mrs. Mulcahey if she's got a light."

"Why do *I* have to go?"

"Cause I said so," Owen began.

"Hey, you two! If Rascal *is* down there, he could be hurt!" I said. We had to get Rascal out right away; Zoe had said we'd better hurry. But how did she know? I decided to worry about that later. *"Come on!"*

"All right, I'll go," Patsy said. "You New Yorkers are so melodramatic!"

It seemed an eternity until she came trudging up the hill with the flashlight.

"Hurry!" I yelled.

"Mrs. Mulcahey wanted to know what we needed it for, but I didn't tell her. I figured she'd think we were daft."

"Oh, you think everybody's daft!" I said impatiently, grabbing the flashlight out of her hand. Before I really thought about what I was doing, I was hanging over the opening, shining the feeble light on stone walls ... mud ... leaves ... twigs ... branches ... more mud ... wait, something moved! It was covered with mud, but— "He's there!" I cried. "I see him, I see him!"

"Where?"

"Let me see!"

"*I* got the flashlight!"

Suddenly we were all peering down the well, and as the light caught his attention, Rascal began to squeal, and so did we, so it sounded like a chorus.

"Go tell Mrs. Mulcahey!"

"We'll need a ladder."

"And a rope."

An hour later, after he'd made the perilous rescue, Owen got to deliver a quivering, squirming Rascal safely into the waiting arms of Mrs. Mulcahey.

"How can I ever thank you children?" she said, wrapping him in a blanket like a newborn baby.

"It was nothing," Owen said modestly.

"We were glad to do it," Gerald chimed in.

"We're just glad that Rascal's safe," Patsy said.

"He's going to need some nourishment, that's for sure," Mrs. Mulcahey said. "And he's shivering fair bad. I'll have Dr. Newton look him over."

"It's just exposure," Zoe said. "He was down there quite awhile." There was something about the way she spoke that made everybody stare at Zoe Mitchell. And she must have realized this because she added "probably" in a not-very-convincing voice.

"Come on, Zoe, take his picture," Gerald said.

And she did then, although Rascal was certainly not looking his best. But neither was Owen.

"You'll need a bath, Owen Parks, and your mum will wonder what you've been up to. If you get a scolding, just tell her you did it for old Mrs. Mulcahey, and there'll be a slab of bacon at her door tomorrow morn."

I started to have second thoughts about the purpose of our rescue mission, but I decided not to ask any questions.

"Thank you!" he said.

As we started the long walk home, I thought how much Owen smelled like our block did one time when a sewer main broke. But I decided not to say anything about that, either.

They had taken all the credit, but I knew who really deserved it. Me, a little, for forcing them to look in the well, but mainly Zoe Mitchell for being so sure he was down there. I kept glancing at her after we'd left the others in the square, but she just kept her head down as if she were counting her steps.

"You were right about us needing the camera, after all," I said. She didn't answer me, so I said, "How'd you know he was down there?"

"I—I heard him squealing."

"No, you didn't. He never squealed at all before we shone the light on him. And you kept saying you could *see* him, not hear him."

"You're *wrong*," she said, shaking her head firmly.

"I am not!" I said. "Please tell me. I can keep a secret. I haven't told anyone about the picture." I knew by the way she looked at me then that the two things were somehow connected.

We were standing in the driveway, and she seemed to be trying to decide whether she could trust me.

"I could just see him down there" was all she said finally.

And I knew it was somehow the truth and that it was all she was able to tell me.

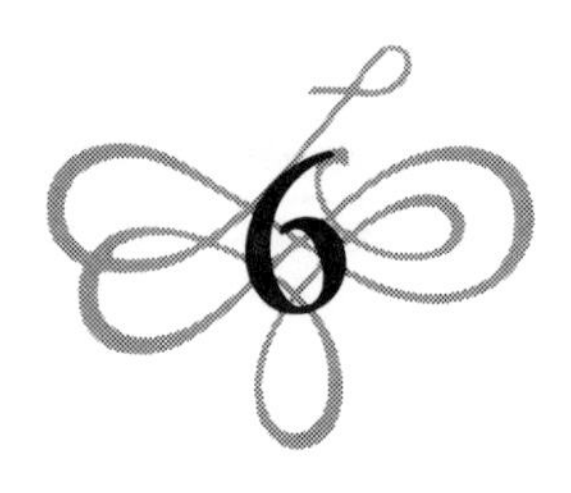

My first impression of Bridget Collins had been almost right. She wasn't exactly a runner; she was a climber. She would go anywhere, anytime, to climb anything. And today, she had informed us at breakfast, we were going with her. We were going to climb Golden Top.

"Golden Top—what's that? It's not a mountain, is it?" I asked, with the natural suspicion of someone who's been raised in an elevator.

"Oh, Cory, of course not. It's but a little bitty thing!" Bridget said.

"Bridget," Zoe said, "it's not *that* little."

"Pshaw. It's hardly worth climbing if you ask me. But I figured as how our guest is a Yankee and was brought up where there's steps to everything, not to mention el-e-va-tors, we should start small."

"Thank you."

"Do we *have* to go?" Zoe asked. "I don't feel so good."

"Yes, we do. And if you got out in the fresh air once in a while, you'd feel a lot better, if you ask me."

"I'm not supposed to go out when it's rainy. Gram's afraid I'll catch cold."

"Well, if you don't go out when it's rainy in these parts, you'll surely be indoors for a good bit of your life, don't you think so, Cory?"

"Uh, I guess so." I didn't want to get in the middle when Bridget and Zoe were going at it, no matter how good-natured it might be. I glanced out the window and it wasn't raining, but it sure looked windy. As if she'd read my mind, Bridget said, "It's a perfect day to climb! It'll fill up your lungs real good, it will!"

And that, it turned out, was that.

We had to drive almost two hours to get to Golden Top because the craggy hilltop was right on the southern coast of England. But finally we were driving down a narrow, winding road and into an area of parked cars. I spotted a huge rock in the center and on it a metal plaque with the words GOLDEN TOP. There was a lot of other writing, something about an Earl Somebody-or-other, but I couldn't make it out. As we got out of the car, with a lot of stretching and groaning, Bridget strode over to a stand where there were maps of the area.

"Here we go," she said heartily, glancing at the map before tucking it into her belt.

She had brought some bug spray, and now she insisted that I spray my arms and legs with it. Zoe did the same and then, with Bridget leading us, we started up the path.

We trudged along in silence for awhile. There were dense trees and bushes on either side and the path was pretty level, so I couldn't see what the big deal was. This wasn't mountain climbing, and there hadn't been any gorgeous scenery so far. I wondered if Zoe was beginning to regret that she'd brought her camera along. It looked as if it would be awfully heavy hanging around your neck. After we had hiked for what seemed like hours, the path began to grow steeper and more difficult. I could tell we were climbing higher because here and there I could spot some light through the trees and catch a quick glimpse of the lush green landscape spreading out below us. Every once in a while Bridget would stop and check the map to make sure we were going the right way.

Finally, when I had grown tired of watching the sweat trickling down Zoe's shirt and of hearing her panting louder and louder as she struggled up ahead of me, I said, "Isn't that thing too heavy? Why did you have to bring it?"

She stopped and slumped against a boulder. "Because I *had* to. I had to take pictures."

"But you haven't taken one. There's no view."

Bridget turned around when we stopped and called down to us, "You two okay? What's the problem?"

"Cory was asking me questions."

"Well, you can chatter at the top."

And with that Zoe bounced up, letting this enormous piece of machinery land what looked like lethal blows on her chest, and plunged on after our leader.

"Come on, keep up," Bridget called down to us. "It's not much farther."

"How can you tell?" I said, now thoroughly out of breath.

"I can see lots of sky. Besides, I have the map, remember?"

She slipped from view for a moment, and then I saw the sky, too. It got bigger and bigger as the trees slipped away, and all of a sudden we had these magnificent views on either side. We weren't actually on Golden Top yet, but we were close, and Zoe began focusing her camera. She stopped and took pictures in several different directions.

"No wonder you lugged that thing along!" I said.

"See?" She smiled this really goofy smile, and it occurred to me it was the first time I'd ever seen her without a serious face.

"Just look around you, girls; have you ever seen anything like this?" Bridget cried. And as I carefully walked a bit closer to the edge, I knew what she was talking about. It was almost like being in an airplane, we were up that high; and down below the whole seacoast lay shining and still and absolutely beautiful.

I backed away a bit and began circling the hilltop, taking in the different views, using my hand to shield my eyes from the blinding sun, while Zoe continued taking pictures.

There were about a dozen other people on the knoll where we were, most of them just stretched out on the grass resting after the climb. The three of us sat down, too, stretching our legs out in front of us and taking swigs from the water bottles that we'd brought along. But after a few moments, Bridget was on her feet again.

"Are we leaving already?" I asked.

"If we want to get the good of the climb, we are," she said.

"What do you mean?"

"Coming up is the easy part," she said. "It's one path straight out and up. Just follow your nose. But going down, there are seven different trails to take. If you plan it right, it should take twice as long because you can zigzag across the whole top! Gives your legs a good workout."

"How do you know which way to go?" Zoe asked. I was glad she was as dumb as I was.

"We have a map, don't we?" Bridget said, slapping it with her hand. "Of course, the more adventurous among us don't use it. We follow our instincts."

I was pretty sure I didn't have any instincts to follow, but I figured they must know that, right? I was used to having a street sign posted at every corner. As Bridget went on and on about things like which side of a tree moss grows on, she lost me completely.

"Anyway," she said, laying her water bottle on the ground with the map while she retied her shoelaces, "we don't want to rest too long. We'll stiffen up!" As she said this, a breeze blew by, lifting the map and dropping it a few feet away. "Whoops, we wouldn't want to lose that, would we?" she said. But as if she'd dared the wind, it suddenly rose in a tremendous gust and the map, despite the three of us lunging after it, sailed off the cliff as gracefully as if we'd folded it into a paper airplane.

"Oh, my word," Bridget said, with a little intake of breath.

"Well, you told us we didn't need it," I said, trying to be cheerful.

She looked at me warily, as if she wasn't sure if I was sincere or being a smart American.

"No, no, of course not," she said. But there was a note of caution in her voice.

We started back down a short while later, and at every bend in the road where two or three little trails branched off, Bridget would call back, "Just follow me, girls. Follow me!" as if she was afraid we were going to be seized by adventure and take off on our own. The whole thing didn't make any sense to me at all. If the trail led straight up, why couldn't it lead straight down? Unfortunately, Bridget was in really good shape, and the distance between us started getting longer and longer. Each time she glanced back and saw us lagging behind, her voice became more impatient.

"Come on, you two. You're old ladies, and that's the truth of it!"

The lower down we got, the thicker the woods became, and it got so we could barely see in front of us. And then suddenly we rounded a bend, and we could see clearly in the distance for the first time in a while. There were three trails, each spreading out in a different direction. It's what Bridget must have meant when she talked about zigzagging across the hilltop. But I was tired, and all I wanted to do was get out of the hot, muggy woods. That's when Zoe spoke.

"Do you see Bridget anywhere?" she asked.

"No," I said, "all the trails are empty!"

Bridget seemed to have vanished. We called out a few times, and at first we could hear her answer as if from a great distance, and then in a few minutes our cries of "Bridget, where are you?" were met by silence, or at most, the chirping of a nearby bird.

Sweat was trickling down my neck and chest. "Are we lost?" I asked Zoe.

"I guess so," she said, in a resigned tone of voice.

"Migod, they'll never find us in here! I hope they put Bridget in prison for a hundred years for this,"

I said, draining the rest of my water bottle. This last dramatic act put me in a feverish thirst, and I thought of all those movies you see where people have to hack their way out of the jungle, and they're almost dead by the time they get back to civilization. (Okay, so maybe—like Patsy said—I'm a little melodramatic.)

Flies and bugs began to swarm around, obviously delighted to have two dinner entrees that were polite enough to stand still.

"Ouch!" I said. "I just got bitten! Come on, Zoe, we can't just stand here. We have to try and catch up with Bridget."

But Zoe Mitchell just leaned against a tree, looking as nonchalant as if she were at a bus stop.

"No, we don't," she said.

"What do you mean?"

"Well, now that we've separated, do you want to just get out of here, I mean, real fast?"

"Are you telling me you know a shortcut?"

"Sort of."

"I thought you'd never been here before."

"I haven't. Promise you won't tell if I get us down out of here *fast?*"

"I promise."

"Then follow me and don't ask any questions."

And with that, Zoe Mitchell hopped up and started rushing down the path to our left, which was the one way I never would have gone. I wanted to yell out, "Are you sure?" but something about the way she'd said "Don't ask any questions" made me shut up. Each time we came to a fork in the road, she didn't even hesitate. We ran as if the wind were chasing us, kicking over rocks and pebbles and laughing as if it were a game. And in what seemed like no time at all, the road got wider and opened up, and we saw the clearing and the parked cars in the distance. We didn't stop till we reached the drinking fountain near the sign where we'd picked up the ill-fated map, and after we'd both taken a long, cold drink, we sank down onto the grass to wait for Bridget.

"What if she went back for us?" I said, beginning to have second thoughts. "What if she thinks we're still up there and doesn't come down, but just keeps looking for us *forever?*" I added, for extra punch.

"I don't think she will. I think she'll know we found our way."

"But how did we?" I asked her then. "How did you know the way? You must have been here before."

"I haven't!"

And when I thought about it, even if she had been here before, it wasn't like finding your way from one street to the next. It was like a jungle, and she'd been like an Indian scout.

"Are you part Indian?" I asked. And we both laughed so hard at my stupid remark that we had to hold our stomachs till they stopped hurting.

"How did you know the way, Zoe? Seriously."

"I don't know," she said. "Really I don't. It's just something I've always been able to do, since I was very little."

"You mean, you have a weird sense of direction or something?"

She shook her head. "That's not it. I can tell which way to go because I can *see* the way. What's crooked for you is straight for me, I guess," she said.

"Sort of like having X-ray vision?"

"Sort of," she said, seeming pleased with the idea.

"Is *that* how you knew where Rascal was? You could see him in the well?"

"Right!" I realized I'd never seen her looking so relaxed, as if it was a relief to be able to talk about whatever this was. "Ever since I was little, when I'd play hide-and-seek with the other kids, I'd always know where everybody was hiding. And I never peeked, honest. But they always thought I did. And then . . ."

"What?"

"Oh, it's nothing."

"Tell me," I pleaded.

"I haven't thought about this for a long time. After we moved to Rose Farm, Gram put me in this private school, and we used to play a game called Hot or Cold. Do you play that in the States?" I nodded. "And I could see where they hid the eraser every time. So the teacher made me go all the way down the hall and wait in another classroom. I remember feeling so bad and wanting to cry because I hadn't peeked and she wouldn't believe me. Anyway, when I went back, I went right over and found the eraser again. I remember it was stuck in with a lot of plants on the windowsill, and the teacher gave me such a look! And after that, she never picked me to be 'it' again. And I was glad because I didn't like the way everybody acted—like I was different."

"Gee, *I* think it's neat."

"You do?"

"Of course I do. You're one of those people who have a special gift."

"Really?"

"Sure. Like this boy in our class who's double-jointed. He's able to touch his nose with his elbow!" I could tell by the look she gave me that she wasn't flattered by the comparison. "What does your grandmother think about it?"

"Oh, that's the trouble. She won't hear of it. That's why you have to promise not to tell."

"I promise, but what do you mean?"

"Well, after that day with the eraser, the teacher said something to Gram about how maybe I should be tested and Gram got real upset. That's when she took me out of the Appleton School and started having me tutored at home. I didn't understand it at the time, but after what happened in the knot garden, I vowed I'd never let her know anything again, ever."

"What happened in the knot garden—and what is that?"

"It's a maze made out of hedges. There's one in Hampton Court. Do you know of it?" I shook my head. "It's sort of a garden, but it's like a puzzle, you know? People get lost in it, and it's tricky to find your way out. It was a big thing with the royals a long time ago; it was the way they amused themselves."

"Well, I guess they didn't have television back then," I said with a straight face, and she giggled.

"Anyway, it was a couple of years after the business at school, and Gram took me to Hampton Court for the day. I remember we had a picnic lunch, and then we went to the maze, but before she could finish explaining to me how difficult it was going to be to find our way out, I had led her straight through to the exit. It upset her something fierce. She kept saying, 'But how did you find the way?' And it was like now, with you, I told her the truth. I said, 'I could just *see* it.' But that made her furious."

"Well, I think it'd be neat to be able to see things the way you do!"

"Oh, you *are* making me feel better! Cause Gram says it's a fault in my character. She says no right-minded person is this way, and I mustn't let anyone know about it. She says if I just ignore it, it will go away. Only it doesn't. And it's getting harder and harder to keep her from knowing when something happens."

"Is that why you stay by yourself all the time and pretend to have headaches?"

"Oh, I'm not pretending!" She seemed annoyed that I would think such a thing. "They're real, all right. It feels sometimes like my head's fair exploding. But Dr. Marsh says it's all in my mind, which makes Gram more convinced than ever that I'm, well, not daft exactly, but what's that word they use—*neurotic,* that's it."

"Well, I don't think you're neurotic. I think you're interesting."

"You really do? You're not just saying that?"

"Of course not."

"But Gram says—"

"Oh, who cares what she says? I'm working on having this really good imagination, and I think anything's possible, you know? And I think it would be really neat to be like you." The endless possibilities of having such a gift raced through my mind while we sat there in silence for a moment. "You must know what's going to be on a test before you even look at it! You know exactly what to study, right?"

She giggled at that, but she didn't get a chance to tell me whether it was true or not because there was a noise in the bushes behind us, and Bridget appeared, looking very frazzled but clearly relieved to see us safe and sound.

"I've been fair sick worried about the two of you! If you hadn't been here, I was going to call the ranger and have them fan out to find you, that I was."

"I'm sure you were, Bridget."

"But how did you ever find your way down?" she persisted.

"Oh, we were just lucky, I guess," Zoe said. Then she did something that really surprised me: She handed Bridget the camera and asked if she would take a picture of the two of us next to the GOLDEN TOP sign. It was only later on that I figured out it was Zoe's way of distracting Bridget and stopping her from asking more questions.

Afterward Bridget still looked frazzled, but all she said was "You're *sure* you're okay?"

"We're fine, aren't we, Cory?"

"Sure," I answered, grinning at her the way I do with Diane when we share a secret. And that's when I realized, with a little surprise, that we really were.

I saw a big change in Zoe Mitchell after the day at Golden Top. She seemed much more relaxed. Some days, especially the rainy ones, we just sat around and watched television together. One afternoon we went to the library, and she let me take some mysteries out on her card; then we went home, and she curled up on one end of the couch and I curled up on the other end and we read all day. It was almost like we were getting to be friends. I asked her about the picture again, but a cloud passed over her face as soon as I mentioned it, so I changed the subject. I guess she just wasn't ready to talk about that yet.

When Wednesday morning dawned nice and sunny, Bridget announced at breakfast that we were going to Stonehenge and Bath. My first thought was that my father would be absolutely thrilled. I'd heard him talk about Stonehenge; with its giant, mysterious stones, it's one of his favorite places, an ancient puzzle that archaeologists love to try and solve. But I'd never heard of Bath.

"What's this Bath place like?" I asked. "That's a weird name."

"Oh, it's a lovely town!" Bridget gushed. "It's got the most wonderful wee shops, and a tearoom where they have delicious apple tarts. And of course," she added, almost as an afterthought, "there are the baths."

"The what?"

"In the Victorian era, they discovered the remains of Roman baths in the town, Cory," Zoe explained. "It became a kind of health spa for the nobility." It was amazing—sometimes Zoe sounded exactly like my parents. It must have been the Cornelia Jessup gene.

We left early, and after a pretty boring drive on a flat, treeless plain (maybe driving with Bridget just *seemed* boring after driving with Jeremiah), suddenly enormous slabs of stone rose up out of nowhere, and I knew we'd arrived at Stonehenge. The stones are arranged in a circle, and there are paths so you can walk around and look up at them, but ropes so you don't get too close. They've been there for a zillion years and nobody can figure out how they got there, or who put them there, or why they're there at all. Right away Zoe started taking pictures.

I was intrigued by the way she handled the camera. It hung by a thick strap around her neck, but her hands always went around the camera itself, cradling it as if it were a living thing that needed protecting, like a baby or a puppy.

"Didn't you say you'd been here before?" I asked her. She nodded, still clicking away. "Then don't you already have enough pictures?"

"Oh, Gram and I were here, but she wouldn't let me bring my camera, so I don't have any photographs."

"Why wouldn't she let you bring your camera?" I asked. Cornelia Jessup just kept getting stranger and stranger, I thought, as I followed Zoe around the different trails.

She was taking a picture of the Heel Stone (naturally she knew the name of everything), and she spoke without moving her eye from the camera lens. "I think it's because it's one of the ways I'm like my mother, and Gram can't abide that. This was my mother's camera, you know," she said, with a hint of pride in her voice.

"Oh, really?" was all I said. I had known that already; I remembered Bridget mentioning it when I'd tried to borrow the camera to take a picture of Rascal. I felt so bad for Zoe that she didn't have a mother, and I wanted to say something about it, but I couldn't think of what to say, so I just stayed quiet. My father told me once that sometimes that's the best thing to do when you don't know what to say. Sometimes I forget and just say something stupid, but sometimes, like now, I remember.

"You don't really see the stones, do you?" she asked me, as she changed the film in her camera.

"Of course I see the stones," I said. Was she calling me stupid?

"No, Cory, maybe you look, but I don't think you really *see.*"

Yep, she was calling me stupid.

"I don't get it. Is this a trick question?"

"What I mean to say is, don't you get an incredible feeling in a place like this? Don't you wish they didn't have all these ropes up? That we could go over and actually touch the stones?"

"Oh yeah, that would be really *neat,*" I said, trying to work up some enthusiasm. I guess I just don't have any sense of history.

When she'd put a fresh roll of film in her camera, Zoe started taking pictures again.

"People used to think it was the Druids that did all this, you know," she called over her shoulder at one point, "but now, of course, they know that it's much, much older than that."

"Of course," I said. Zoe Mitchell was really beginning to get on my nerves. It was like the worst class trip I'd ever been on. But Bridget had stopped to listen to a tour guide, so I figured I had no choice but to follow her around and pretend to be listening while I waited for things to pick up.

I didn't have long to wait.

Something had gone wrong, but I thought at first it was just the camera. Zoe had lifted it up to her eye to focus on a shot and then dropped it quickly, as if it had burned her hand. Then, as the camera lay against her chest looking curiously abandoned, she started backing away from the rope that was guarding the stones. She seemed to be searching for something in the distance, because as I hurried over to her, I could see her eyes were wide and kind of scary.

"Zoe, what happened?"

She didn't answer me, but stopped and just stood there, shaking her head back and forth as if she were feeling dizzy. Then she started doing the strangest thing of all: She started shivering.

"You're *cold?*" I said with a giggle, because the day was humid and warm and everybody had been talking about how unusual that was for England.

Again she ignored me, but she started moving again, turning her back on me and going farther and farther away from the center of the monument. I didn't follow her because it was clear I wasn't wanted, and I was beginning to have that old feeling about Zoe again. Whatever friendship I thought we'd begun seemed to have vanished. Then suddenly, without turning around, she called out, "Cory ..." in a small, frightened voice that sent chills all through me. I went over to where she was standing and found her still shivering, with her eyes squeezed shut.

"I'm here, Zoe. What's *wrong?*"

She didn't answer for a moment, but when she opened her eyes, she looked relieved to see me.

"I'm so glad you're here," she said in the same soft voice that made her sound like a little kid.

"Of course I'm here. What happened?"

"Nothing." Nothing? Now she was attempting a smile. "Actually, I think I got away in time!"

"Huh?"

"Let's go back inside, okay?"

By inside I guessed she meant the gift shop, where they sold the guidebooks, postcards, and other souvenirs.

"Shouldn't we wait for Bridget?" I said, looking around until I finally spotted her on the other side.

"She'll know where to find us," she said, and without waiting, she started running back to the parking lot where the shop was located.

I hurried after her. When I reached the gift shop, I found her inside, leaning against the wall, out of breath. She still had her arms folded across her chest, as if there'd been a chill and she'd forgotten to bring her sweater.

"Zoe, are you sick or something?"

She didn't answer me right away. Then she took a deep breath.

"No, I'm fine now; it's okay," she said finally.

"You sure?"

She looked at me, and I could tell she was putting on a big act, but I didn't say anything. "I'm fine. Really I am. You want to get some postcards?"

"Aren't you going to take any more pictures?"

"No, I want to save some film for Bath."

She seemed to get calmer as we spoke, and I had a hunch it was like the photograph—she just wasn't going to talk about it—so I went over to look at the postcards. Even though I'd already sent some with pictures of the Lion's Head Inne to Diane and a few of my other friends back home, I figured I'd get one to keep as a souvenir.

Two boys came over and started looking at the postcards the same time as I did.

"Willie and me been here before, and we figured the whole thing out," the taller one said.

"You did not!"

"Sure we did. If you wasn't so stupid, you'd see it, too."

"I am not stupid. My pop says no one knows nothin' about how they got here."

"Well, *we* do."

Zoe had joined me at the postcard stand, and she shot me a look when she heard the conversation.

"What was it you figured out?" she asked the boy.

He stared at her for a moment, as if deciding if she looked suspicious.

"Dinosaurs, that's what we figured," he answered

finally. Then, maybe afraid he was being too polite, he added, "Not that it's any of your business."

"Dinosaurs?"

"Sure, you know about them, don't you? They was big, huge monsters. They could have lifted stones like them *easy.* That's why they're arranged so badly. If it were men who'd done it, they'd be a bit neater, in rows or such, don't you think?"

Zoe let out a giggle, which seemed to infuriate the boy but made me feel much better. Whatever had happened out there was over, and she was nice and relaxed again. The thought crossed my mind that maybe Zoe Mitchell was just plain crazy, but since she was all I had to hang around with over here, I decided not to believe that. Strange and eccentric maybe. And gifted, in that weird way we'd talked about.

Now she fixed her attention on the boy. "It couldn't be dinosaurs," she explained patiently. "The nearest age most archaeologists have come up with is the early monolithic Bronze Age."

Could I have the crazy Zoe back, please?

The boy looked at her and sneered. "A lot *you* know," he said, stomping off.

Zoe poked me with her elbow and giggled, and I knew she was trying to let me know that I could relax because whatever it was was over. For now, anyway.

When I finally got around to picking a postcard, I chose a photograph that had been taken at night.

It had a really spooky look to it, so I figured after I was back home it would help me remember the strange things that had happened here.

When it was all over, of course, I wouldn't need any souvenirs to remind me. But I didn't know that yet. If I had, I would have saved my money.

We finally got to Bath, and I knew when we drove down this long, winding hill and saw the town in the distance that I was going to like Bath better than Stonehenge. For one thing, Bridget was right; it was a very pretty town, with gardens full of flowers and lots of little shops and finally (I was starved) a really good lunch. Then, just when I was enjoying myself, Bridget said we had to go and take a tour of the baths.

Our guide was a tiny woman with gray hair who kept holding up a closed red umbrella so our group wouldn't start following another guide by mistake. We trudged through one old building after another, and when I say old, believe me, we're talking *old.*

"As we leave the museum," she was saying, "we are faced with the most impressive feature of the

Roman baths, the Great Bath, discovered in 1878 . . ."

"I'm no history person, but this sure looks older than that," I whispered to Zoe.

She turned and looked at me the way my mother does sometimes. It was that archaeological gene surfacing again, I could tell.

"It was *discovered* then, Cory. It dates from Roman times."

"I knew it!" I said. "From the time when there were gladiators, like in *Spartacus,* right?" She nodded, but her forehead was getting a little crease in it as if I were some kind of problem she wasn't able to solve.

We kept trudging through these old buildings with these baths that had just sprung up out of nowhere, which is where they got the name of the town. That much I figured out. Only they kept saying, like Zoe did, how when they discovered these baths from Roman times, all the rich people started coming to them and turned it into a health spa. Now, I have to tell you these baths were filled with green, murky water and I, for one, would never bathe in water that looked like that. You had to come out much dirtier than when you went in. It was even worse than the Hudson River, and that's pretty bad.

The guide was going on and on, and steam kept rising from the baths, and it was getting so humid

I began to feel like I was on the subway at rush hour in July and the air-conditioning had broken down. Zoe was clicking away again, turning this way and that, taking shots from every angle. But as we all started to leave to go into another room, I realized she wasn't following. In fact, she wasn't moving at all. Bridget and the others went through to the next part, but Zoe was still standing by the pool, staring at some stone steps over in the corner. She had stopped holding the camera, and it just dangled by the strap around her neck. Her hands hung limply by her side.

Oh, no, not again!

"Zoe, you okay?"

No answer.

I tried to tell myself that she couldn't hear me over the noise of the other tourists as they shuffled out of the room, so I went over and lightly tapped her on the arm. That's when I really got what Gerald called the heebie-jeebies, because in this warm, humid place her arm was like ice, and this time I felt it, too. There was a coldness all around us, as if I had just stepped into this little circle of air-conditioning. Even though I'd been hot and sweaty a minute ago, I hated the coldness. As I moved around to look at Zoe's face, I remembered her shivering at Stonehenge. Now I saw her eyes still focused blankly on the steps. "Zoe, answer me! What's wrong?" I touched her lightly again, and this time she stirred, blinking and looking at me as if she'd just been taking a nap and couldn't remember where she was for a minute.

"What's the matter, Cory?" she said, with a little shiver.

"There's nothing the matter with me, but what just went on with *you?*" She rubbed her forehead then, and her eyes, as if to clear her vision. "Are you okay?"

She glanced at me for a moment before she spoke. "Yes, I'm fine. Why do you ask?"

"Because you were standing there, kind of in a trance, you know?" I laughed when I said it because the words just tumbled out, but that's exactly what it was like. "What was happening to you?"

I realized I was backing away from her as we spoke, to get back into the safety of nice, warm air and away from the chill of where Zoe was standing.

She shook her head. "Nothing," she said, as Bridget appeared in the archway.

"Girls, the guide is waiting for you. We all have to stay together!"

"Uh, you go ahead, Bridget," I said. "I turned my ankle. We'll just wait for you outside on the benches, okay?"

"Oh, dear, are you hurt?" she said, looking really upset.

"No, no, I'm fine," I assured her. "Go ahead."

"Well, all right, then. Cheerio! But wait right

outside. I don't want to lose you again like I did on Golden Top!"

I nodded to reassure her, and she hurried away to catch up with the others.

After we'd reached the benches outside, Zoe and I sat in silence for a few moments. Finally I couldn't stand it any longer. "What was going on in there, Zoe?" I demanded. "And don't tell me *nothing!*"

"I'd tell you if I could, Cory, but you'd only think me—"

"Daft?"

Her head jerked up then, and she looked at me with a really frightened expression on her face. "I am *not!*"

"I know you're not. I was only kidding. That's Gerald's favorite word."

"I'm just so tired of it . . ." she said.

"Tired of what, Zoe? Tell me!"

"Seeing things!" She blurted out the words, but the effort seemed to have a calming effect on her, as if the worst was over now.

"What kind of things do you see?" I asked, not really sure I wanted to know.

"Cory, when I'm in a place that's very old, I can see what went on there a long time ago. It's almost as if the things that happened and people's feelings at the time don't leave. They stay there, like cobwebs clinging to the walls. Sometimes it's only shadows; but other times I see *real people.*"

"People? What kinds of people?"

"Well, just now these men were sitting on the steps, and they were wrapped in some kind of big towels. And I think they had cups in their hands."

I swallowed hard. Okay, I *know* I keep bragging about having that great imagination. But to tell you the truth, it's got to have some limits.

"You think I'm crazy, don't you?"

"I do not. Don't say that!"

"I shouldn't have told you any of this. But you made me feel so much better the other day." Oh, God, she was really crying now, and I wanted to die. "I've never really had a friend, Cory. And I thought maybe you were becoming one."

"I *am.*" I *am?* "Just calm down and give me a minute. Remember, you've had a while to think about this, but it's the first time I've heard of such a thing except in ghost stories."

"Do you think that's what they are? You think I'm seeing ghosts?"

She was back to being calm again, like she was saying, "You think I should have a ham on rye or pumpernickel?"

"I don't know. But if they're people who are dead already, that's what they're called, right?"

"Right," she agreed, nodding. "I was thinking the other day," she went on, "maybe it's like you said, I have this kind of X-ray vision, and that's why I can see them. Do you think that's what it is, Cory?"

"Could be!" I said. What else could I say? "Let's see, what do we already know? One, we know that you could see Rascal in the well long before anybody knew he was there. I mean, you told me that we would need the camera, remember, when we weren't even near the well. Two, you knew how to get us down from Golden Top; three, I saw you in the baths. You were like a marble statue in there, Zoe; something was going on. Tell me *exactly* what happens."

I was beginning to warm up to the whole thing. It was a lot more interesting than the mystery novel I'd been trying to get through yesterday!

"It starts like a kind of buzzing . . . real soft, you know. As if someone's trying to get through to me on a radio. No, that's not it, exactly. It's just a feeling I get. Like when you can tell someone's staring at you in a crowd. Yeah, that's it! And I get cold. I always start to shiver."

"Is that what was happening at Stonehenge?"

She nodded, but she seemed so eager to talk about it now that I decided I'd better not interrupt again to tell her that in the baths I had felt the cold, too. (Did that make me some kind of accomplice?)

"When it happens, I feel a kind of mood," she went on. "Like sometimes it's very sad, and other times it's scary, as if there was a bad fight in the place a long time ago. Cory, remember I told you how I try so hard to ignore it? That doesn't seem to be working anymore. I was able to make it stop at

Stonehenge, but in the baths it was stronger than ever. The people were clearer than I've ever seen them before. But at least this time they were laughing. They were definitely happy."

"Why do you think it's getting stronger?" I asked.

"I'm not sure. Maybe because Gram's not around? Ever since the picture, I've avoided places like these."

"There you are!" Bridget's voice boomed out behind us. Oh, no, go back in! I want to find out about the picture! "I must tell you you missed a most remarkable tour. But more important, how would the ankle be now?"

"Oh, fine, Bridget. Just fine."

"Well, good; then we'd best be on our way. Would you like to get a postcard, Cory?"

"Yes, I would."

"We'll stop on the way to the parking spaces, then."

I picked one of the Great Bath where Zoe said she saw the men, and I got a chance to look at it a lot on the ride home. There was no one to talk to because Bridget liked to concentrate on her driving, and as soon as we'd reached the car, Zoe seemed to collapse. She just climbed into the backseat, curled up with her head on her sweater, and slept like a baby all the way home.

I glanced over at her once, and she looked like someone who'd just taken a long, hard journey. And I think maybe she had. But to *where?*

When we arrived home that evening, there was a message from Cornelia saying that she and my parents would be arriving back in Olbourne sometime the next afternoon. It might have been my imagination, but I thought I could actually see Zoe go into a little slump when Bridget read the news. I guess I'd go into a slump, too, if I knew I was off to Headache City again.

They pulled into the driveway about five o'clock the next day, with Cornelia looking so nervous as she got out of the car that I almost started to laugh. But she seemed to feel much better as soon as the engine was turned off, and soon she was bustling back and forth, collecting her bags and talking on and on about the conference, and how good it was to be home again, and how she would never, ever go away again. The more she talked, the more Zoe seemed to droop, like a plant that someone has left unwatered on a windowsill. Then Cornelia thanked me profusely for keeping her granddaughter company—as if that were such an unusual thing—and retreated through the kitchen door with Zoe, pulling the door shut behind her.

When I heard the key turn in the lock, I got a little chill down my spine.

The next morning my father drove my mother to the library in nearby Spindle to finish up some research, while I sat restlessly switching channels and listening to the pounding of rain on the roof as it drowned out the sound of the television. The most awful storm had been raging all morning, and I felt trapped. Every once in a while I got up to press my nose against the window and prayed for it to clear. I was used to being independent, being able to hop on a bus or a subway anytime I wanted. But in Olbourne—even without the rain—what could I do? Hop a cow? I tried to get interested in *The Mystery at Briar Ridge,* but my thoughts kept wandering to the other mystery, the real-life one, that was going on right next door. I realized with a start that I actually missed Zoe Mitchell and wanted to go to the kitchen door like a little kid and ask, "Can Zoe come out to play?" But somehow I knew that since old Cornelia was back, Zoe couldn't come out and play anymore.

I thought what fun it would be to just barge right in there and get it all cleared up:

Cornelia, *what* is your problem? Why are you making Zoe's life so miserable? Bad enough she lost a really neat-sounding mother and is stuck in this dead town with you and tutors. Do you have to make her think she's going nuts, too? So she's a little eccentric—big deal!

When I went into the kitchen to make a snack, I could hear Zoe and her grandmother moving around in there, and it gave me the creeps.

At noon the sound of the postman's van on the gravel driveway made me jump up and run to the door. (It was the kind of day when the arrival of the mail was exciting.) I was about to go out and get it when I heard the other door open and, peeking out the window, I saw Zoe come out, shielded by a huge black umbrella, and run to the mailbox. I watched as she emptied the contents of their silver box into a bag she was carrying. Then she opened our mailbox and emptied that, too. I stepped back from the window, hiding behind the curtain a bit so she wouldn't see me, while she ran back up the driveway to the house. Then I heard our doorbell ring.

I opened the door, and she was standing there like a lost puppy, handing me the mail with a shy grin on her face.

"Thank you," I said. "You didn't have to do that."

"Well, I was getting our mail anyway. I figured I'd save you a trip. It's so awful out."

As she said this, I became aware that large puddles were forming around her feet. It was the kind of downpour that came at you from the side, slashing you with huge stabs of rain that soaked you clear through in no time flat. It wasn't warm like the summer rain we had at home, which I only remembered when Zoe let a big shiver run through her.

"You want to come in?" I asked.

Of course not. She'd much rather stay out there until the floodwaters reach her armpits.

"Thanks," she said, rushing past me so quickly that her slicker got my arm all wet. "I guess I'd better take my shoes off or I'll ruin the carpet." She hung her slicker on one of the hooks by the door and pulled a white envelope out of the mail sack. She seemed really excited.

"I got some of the pictures back from Golden Top," she said. "Would you like to see them?"

"Sure, bring them over here where you can spread them out," I said, thinking as we moved into the dining room how glad I was that she had come over. She looked at the snapshots first and then, one by one, she handed them to me. Most of them were scenic views, and they were very nice, but to tell you the truth, I don't know if they were really good or not. They *looked* pretty good to me; they weren't blurry, and nobody in them had two heads. And nobody in them had just dropped in from another century.

"They're very good," I said.

"They are, aren't they?" she said, her eyes shining.

"You really like to take pictures, don't you?"

She nodded, as if the words were too dangerous to be spoken out loud. "Sometimes I think the only time I can see clearly is through the camera."

Suddenly there were two sharp raps on the kitchen door, and then Cornelia's voice, muffled but clear, called out, "Zoe? Are you in there? Where's the mail, child!"

Zoe jumped and began to stuff the pictures back in the envelope.

"Do you want me to go to the door?" I asked. She shook her head, but she looked so miserable that suddenly I got angry. "Don't let her push you around!"

"It's all right; I should go. I shouldn't have bothered you in the first place. They're stupid pictures . . ." She was mumbling now and rushing to the door, the envelope with the pictures shoved into the bag with the rest of the mail.

"Wait," I said, going after her. As she opened the door, she almost collided with her grandmother, who was standing there like a bank guard.

"I have your lunch waiting, Zoe." Then to me, "Hello, Cory."

Somehow the way she said "hello" made it sound more like "good-bye."

I hope you can picture the scene: Zoe, her grandmother, and me squished together as if we were trapped in a revolving door. Cornelia didn't move, but stood like a sentry by the door; I was standing on our side of the doorway, and Zoe was sandwiched between us like a piece of salami.

"Can Cory have lunch with us?" she asked suddenly.

"Oh, no, that's too much trouble," I began, like I always do when I'm at Diane's house and she invites me to stay.

"It's no trouble," Zoe said. (Notice Zoe was saying this, not Cornelia.)

"Perhaps Cory has other plans," her grandmother said, with a weak little smile like she wasn't dying to slam the door in my face. What was wrong with this woman?

"No, no, I have no plans. In fact, I was just about to fix myself something." I don't know what made me so pushy all of a sudden!

"Then Cory *can* have lunch with us, can't she, Gram?" It was like Zoe and I were doing the same thing, trying to puncture Cornelia's coat of armor, but probably for totally different reasons. I think Zoe just wanted someone as a buffer against the old lady. I know I sure would.

"Well, of course," Cornelia said, finally stepping back from the door so Zoe and I could pass through.

Cornelia had set the table in the dining room, and once again I felt I had to make some protest. "Oh, I'm intruding, really," I began, but then Zoe gave me a look—not unlike the kind that Diane and I exchanged back home, which said, *don't you dare desert me now!*—so I let my voice trail off while Cornelia Jessup went and got another plate.

It was some kind of meat she was serving, not in a sandwich, but just on a plate with bread and butter on the side, and a salad that I think is their version of potato salad. It had a lot more vinegar in it than the kind we get at home.

"So, are you enjoying your vacation in the British Isles?" Cornelia began. Why did I feel as if I might be graded on my answer?

"It's been really nice," I said. "It's a pretty country, England."

"It's your first trip abroad, isn't it?"

"Yep."

"Pity."

There was a pause while I absorbed this rebuke. I'm only eleven years old, I wanted to say; you expect me to be a world traveler? But then I realized that her granddaughter was almost a world traveler. Maybe that's what she considered the norm. I turned to Zoe.

"You've traveled a lot, haven't you?"

She had her mouth full of the sour potato salad, and it took her a minute to answer.

"I used to travel a lot, when I was little ... with my mum."

"More meat, Cory?" Cornelia interrupted.

"No, thank you. Where have you been?"

"Oh, all different places. I don't even remember most of them, but I do remember Cairo, that was one of the last ones, and Madrid—"

"Zoe, you must not talk when you're eating. It interferes with the digestion."

"I don't think it does," I said, suddenly bold. "My father always says that good conversation helps the digestion because it relaxes the stomach muscles." (Did he really say that?)

Cornelia glared at me.

"Well, Zoe is a very slow eater, so it's better that she concentrate on her plate."

We all finished our meal in silence then, and I watched carefully as Zoe put her fork down and chewed and swallowed her last bite of food.

"I guess you've seen most of England, too, I'll bet."

"Not really," Zoe said quietly.

"How come?"

Zoe shrugged her shoulders then, but looked at me with her head turned to one side like a cocker spaniel. She wore a look of confusion, as if she didn't know what I wanted her to say. And no wonder. *I* didn't know what I wanted her to say. Looking back on it, I think I just wanted Cornelia Jessup to know that she wasn't fooling anybody by keeping Zoe locked up all the time. People noticed—*I* noticed. But I guess she didn't feel too threatened by a kid from New York who would be gone in a few days because she rose from the table and began to clear the dishes, ignoring us completely.

"It's really a shame you don't get out more," I said. "Someone as *nice* and *normal* as you should be out in the village with people, singing and dancing, every day." All right, so I got carried away, but my intentions were good. There was a loud clatter at the sideboard as Cornelia dropped some cups and saucers.

"Cory Gales, you are an impudent child. What are you doing, trying to upset Zoe?"

Zoe's face had turned white as a ghost's, and my stomach did a little flip-flop. Whether from boredom or curiosity, or just trying to help Zoe, I had gone too far. But also too far to turn back.

"Why? What did I say that would upset Zoe?"

She glared at me, and I don't know why I wasn't more afraid. I just stared back. I knew I was being fresh, but I tried hard not to look *too* fresh.

"Don't be cross with Cory, Gram; she's my friend—my first *friend*," she said, and tears welled up in her eyes.

"Go to your room, Zoe."

Zoe's lip began to tremble, and I felt sick to my stomach. "Listen, I'm sorry. Let's just change the subject. Okay? Talk about something else?"

"Why is it, Cory, that I don't think you're interested in anything else?"

"Oh, but I am. Let's talk about Olbourne. You have a really pretty village here."

Zoe looked like she was going to throw up as I went on about the gardens and the pretty fountain, and then I made the mistake of singing the praises of the Lion's Head Inne and the lovely Parks family. I mean, I've hardly ever even been in there, and okay, maybe I *was* making a teeny tiny dig at her thinking she was so much better than everybody else in the village, but it wasn't planned or anything. Anyway, that really set old Cornelia off.

"What have those little urchins in the village been telling you? A lot of nonsense? I hope you realize when you're in a . . . a certain position, as I am, people feel the need to gossip about you. Anything you might have heard is simply that—gossip. And I'm sure however threadbare your upbringing has been, you have been taught not to spread gossip or listen to it."

"I don't think my upbringing has been threadbare," I said quietly.

"You don't have to be insulting to our guest, Gram," Zoe said, seeming suddenly to have found the strength to speak up to Cornelia.

Cornelia took a deep breath and seemed to be holding it for a moment, and I wondered crazily if she was going to get beet red like little kids do sometimes when they're trying to get their own way. But slowly she let it out.

"Perhaps I owe you an apology, Cory. I did not intend to insult you."

"That's all right. I . . . I didn't mean to upset either of you," I said, glancing nervously from one to the other. It was obvious now that Zoe was more composed than her grandmother.

"Cory's right, Gram. The Parks children are nice. I . . . I went to Mrs. Mulcahey's with them and Gerald McCray while you were gone." I have heard the term "breathing fire" to describe someone who was so angry they looked like a dragon. Now I saw it happening right in front of me. Cornelia Jessup's eyes were fairly bulging out of her head, and she was staring so intently at her granddaughter that I expected to see Zoe begin to melt, like the wicked witch in *The Wizard of Oz.* But Zoe Mitchell was full of surprises. "And I brought my camera, and I took pictures. At Mrs. Mulcahey's and at Golden Top. And . . ."

"Zoe! I think you should go to your room."

Zoe did melt then and got up to put her plate on the sideboard. I stood up, too, but I looked at Cornelia Jessup and thought, You're just a bully, like Billy Larson was in second grade. Only you're old and you wear a dress!

"I don't know what this is all about, Mrs. Jessup, but you surely have made me curious. That's all you're doing, you know, feeding the gossip mill." (That was an expression I'd heard at home on one of those talk shows I watched when my parents weren't around.)

"Lunch is over, Cory" was all Cornelia Jessup said. I was being thrown out! What would my mother say?

"Thank you very much," I said, feeling suddenly shaky. "It was delicious."

At that there was a soft rap on the door, and we heard my father's voice.

"Excuse me, Cornelia? Is Cory in there with you?"

There was a second of hesitation while the three of us stood still, all probably with the same thought: Had they heard anything? Then Cornelia went and opened the door.

"Good afternoon, Jeremiah. Yes, Cory's been visiting us for lunch. She was just leaving, in fact."

"How nice of you, Cornelia!" he said in his booming voice.

"Is it still as nasty out?" she asked him.

"Beginning to slow down. Weather forecast says it'll blow out to sea tomorrow, and it should be a lovely weekend." My father looked at me. "Which means we're spending the weekend in London, young lady. Would you like that?"

"I'd love it!" I said, inching my way to the door.

As I squeezed myself around my father—who persisted in acting like Mr. Rogers, smiling and chatting with his neighbor—I heard him say, "Zoe, would you like to come with us? I think Cory would enjoy it more being with someone her own age."

"I don't think so, Jeremiah; thank you anyway," Cornelia answered. "You are very kind."

"Gram, I want to go!"

"Oh, do let her come, Cornelia. It's the least we can do after she's entertained Cory all this time."

"I don't think so. It would be an imposition on you and your family."

"Please, Gram! Cory *wants* me to go. Don't you, Cory?"

"Sure, we all want her to go, Mrs. Jessup. It'll be good because she can show us around all those *old* places."

What can I tell you? Torturing Cornelia Jessup was turning into a hobby.

Anyway, she finally had to say yes. And my father worked out the details with the nice, friendly, fire-breathing dragon lady. Zoe would be all packed and ready to go by eight the next morning.

But I wasn't sure *I* would be. Lying in bed that night, I began to consider the possibilities. What would happen when we had Zoe away from Cornelia for a whole weekend, with her camera, just boppin' from one old ruin to another?

It was too terrible to think about.

"Tickets if you will, miss."

I handed over the two tickets that I'd kept zippered securely in my jacket pocket and watched as the conductor punched each one carefully.

Across the aisle and two rows down, my mother was already staring out the window, enjoying the scenery while my father sat steeped in some paperback he'd brought along to read on the journey into London. When the conductor returned the ticket stubs, I placed them back in the pocket of my windbreaker and settled back to look out the window and watch the green fields and cottages and farms that were passing by. Zoe Mitchell was sitting opposite me with her forehead pressed against the glass. Neither of us had spoken very much so far this morning, and now I began to wonder why she was so absorbed in the passing scenery. She should be used to cows, and sheep in the meadow, and cottages with thatched roofs. They should be everyday things to her. Then, as I continued watching her, I began to realize that she wasn't really seeing anything. At least not anything on the other side of the window. I could tell that her mind was miles away, and I began to wonder where it was and what it was seeing. I'm not sure why, but it didn't seem to be ordinary daydreaming she was doing, and that really creepy feeling began to steal over me again.

I had been thinking a lot about what she'd told me, and one part of me said, It's a special gift, and it must be really neat at exam time. But another part of me said, It must be the pits to go around bumping into people who've already been dead for a hundred years.

We pulled into the train station just after nine o'clock and shuffled along the platform slowly, blending in with all the other people going into the city. I began to get a rush of excitement. Finally we were in London and going to see things I'd always heard about. Famous things, things I'd seen in movies and on television!

We took a short bus ride to Covent Garden and spent some time poking in and out of the little shops that filled the area. I bought a pair of tiny bird earrings for Diane and a bangle bracelet for myself. Zoe looked at everything, but she didn't buy anything. She had the camera with her, of course, and she stopped every ten seconds to take pictures.

After a while, we headed back to the center of London, to see the changing of the guard at Buckingham Palace. It happens every day at the same time, and it was hard to see over the heads of all the other tourists who had come to watch and had formed a mob outside the gates. It was kind of neat to see something up close and real that I'd only seen in photographs or in the movies. Up until now, I think part of me didn't really believe places like Buckingham Palace actually existed. Standing there, I felt myself changing—not a lot, maybe only an inch or so—but I think I began to understand why people like to travel so much.

By now I was getting hungry, and I was glad when my parents suggested we all have lunch at a tearoom nearby. But when we got there, it was so crowded that we had to split up. My parents took a table in the rear while Zoe and I waited as a well-dressed couple at a table near the door kept talking and talking. The New Yorker in me was beginning to surface, and I had to stifle the urge to go over and say, "You've finished your lunch, and you've paid your check, so why are you still using this table? We're starved!" I found it hard to believe that the waitress would let them *do* such a thing! Sometimes the English are just too polite, if you ask me.

Finally they got up and left, and we slid into the seats and started looking over the menu. I decided on the shepherd's pie and sat looking out the window after giving my order to the waitress. I had gotten used to ordering shepherd's pie because I liked the mashed potatoes on top and the way the meat and the gravy all sort of mushed together. And it wasn't as strange as some of the things on the menu, one of which I'd just heard Zoe order.

The shop was on a corner, and it was interesting to watch all the people go by and the traffic whiz back and forth. Instead of having traffic lights at the intersections, they had these zebra lines painted across. I was fascinated at the brave way people would just step off the curb and walk boldly to the other side, trusting that the cars and especially the trucks (or lorries, as they called them here) would screech to a halt. If you did that in Manhattan, you'd be a grisly statistic before you got halfway across the street.

"So, what did you order?" I asked brightly, as if I hadn't just heard her order something that made me want to barf.

"Beef and kidney pie," she said.

"Do you really *like* that?" I asked. Of course not—she's ordered it as some kind of penance.

"Sure I do," she said, giggling. "You don't have meat pies in the States, do you?"

I shook my head. "We have Big Macs."

"Oh, well, we have those here, too, you know," Zoe said, nodding out the window.

I turned and looked over my shoulder and sure

enough, down at the end of the narrow, winding street, there was a McDonald's. My mouth began to water, but it was already too late. Our pies had arrived.

I finished before Zoe did because I just wolfed it down, and then I sat watching her eat like a delicate little bird. No wonder she was so thin. Or maybe she really didn't like beef and kidney pie, after all. Maybe her grandmother made her eat it: "Anytime you go into a tearoom for lunch, you *must* order beef and kidney pie!"

"So how long have you lived with your grandmother?" I asked.

"About five years now."

"Well, Olbourne seems like a nice place to live," I said.

She nodded. "It's all right."

"If you got to hang around with the other kids, I think you'd like it more," I said, knowing it was a pretty dumb thing to say.

"But Gram wouldn't like that."

"Oh, for gosh sakes!" I stopped before I said something really mean because, after all, this *was* her grandmother, and as far as I knew, the only relative she had in the whole world. I thought fleetingly of my two grandmothers and my Aunt Dottie and my Uncle Bob, and I was so glad that they were around. I mean, they don't live right next door, and we don't even see them very much, but at least I know they're out there somewhere.

"What has she got against the Parks kids?" I asked.

"I don't know. I think it's just that they don't like us. You know, because we live in the manor house."

"There seem to be so many things she won't let you do," I said, trying to be tactful. I thought how much freedom my folks gave me, and I made a little mental note to be grateful for that when I got home. "I still don't understand why she doesn't like you using the camera."

"I told you, it was my mother's."

"I know, I know, but your mother was her daughter. I mean . . ." A thought suddenly hit me: My mother had said that Cornelia and her daughter didn't get along, and she had called Rachel "a bit of an eccentric." "Zoe, do you think your mother was . . . like you? I mean, do you think she had the same . . . gift?"

She looked at me for a moment, and from the way her eyes opened wide, I could tell that she had never thought about that. Then she smiled.

"Oh, I hope so," she said. "That would be lovely, wouldn't it?"

I wondered what she meant by that, but the waitress had started hovering over us, waiting to give us the check.

"You want some dessert?" I asked.

"No, thank you," she said, carefully wiping her mouth with her napkin like a proper English lady. "I think we'd better go. Your parents are waiting."

We took a boat up the Thames River to get to the Tower of London, and Zoe and I hung over the side of the boat, despite my mother's warnings, and let the spray hit us in the face. It was icy cold, and it felt good.

I always imagined that the Tower would be one building, and it would be high and spooky, because that's where everybody—even members of the royal family—lost their heads in the old days. But it's not like that at all. We came up a cobblestone path into a clearing where there were lots of stone buildings, almost like a village. A soft breeze was blowing, and the sun was shining brightly as we joined a tour led by one of those guards you've seen pictures of, the ones wearing the fancy uniforms and the big hats.

At first I couldn't believe Zoe had never been here before, but then I realized there are lots of places in New York that tourists always see and that I've never been to. I guess when you live in a place, you figure you don't have to cram everything into a week or so, and you end up never seeing anything. Unless, of course, you have visitors from out of town, and you take them.

I soon discovered that Zoe was a reader; she read every sign and every little plaque she saw, just like my parents. It didn't surprise me; it was the old Jessup gene again. But she was even slower than my parents, and we were soon way behind them on the tour.

It was kind of fun, trudging up stairs and over

ramps and visiting places that had been there for centuries. We don't have that sort of thing in New York. Where I live, if you blink, a building's gone and two minutes later another one is put up in its place.

We climbed up to a tiny, dark space that's called the Bloody Tower, and the Yeoman guide started telling us about this man named Sir Walter Raleigh who was imprisoned in the tower for twelve years! The room was furnished just as it had been when he was there, with a copy of a book called *History of the World* on a desk. It was a book he had actually written while in prison. (I think I'd be too busy sulking, or thinking how I was going to get even when I got out, to sit down and write the whole history of the world.) By now, I was beginning to feel as if I were on a class trip again, so when the guide stopped talking, I turned eagerly and began to follow the others down the narrow, twisting stone steps. I had gotten about halfway down, the spiral staircase making my head spin, when I realized Zoe wasn't behind me. I turned and went back up—with a sinking feeling that I knew what was keeping her.

I was right; it was the same as before. Only this time she was standing staring at a stone wall.

I started to touch her arm, but again I felt the cold and backed away.

"Zoe, are you okay?"

She didn't answer me, and I began to get really spooked. The hair stood up on my neck. I'd always heard that expression, but I'm here to tell you that it really does happen. Finally, I poked her, and she moved a little, and, keeping her eyes lowered, turned as if to follow me back down.

I stood blocking her way to the stairs until she finally raised her eyes, but they were like the eyes of a doll I once had, all glassy and blank, and while she was staring right at me, she seemed to be staring right *through* me.

"It's okay, Zoe. I'm here with you. Tell me what's going on."

She seemed to wake up then, as if she'd been in a trance, and realized where she was and who I was.

"Oh, God, Cory, why is this happening to me? Suddenly, it's happening all the time!"

And with that, she shoved me aside and clumped down the stairs so fast that I had to hurry to catch up with her. When we came out into the fresh air, I grabbed her arm and spun her around.

"What was it this time, Zoe?"

But she was in control again, and all she said was "I'm okay now and I don't want to talk about it. There's your mother and father. We'd better not keep them waiting."

I hurried after her because I had no choice, and after we'd caught up with my parents, neither of us talked about it anymore.

But every once in a while, I would remember that tonight I would be sharing a room with Zoe Mitchell. And I couldn't help wondering . . . who *else?*

Mrs. Fairworthy's Bed and Breakfast was a little white house, one in a row of seven, with bright red geraniums tumbling out of its shiny black window boxes and a giant brass doorknocker on the door. Our room was two flights up at the top of the stairs. It was small, with twin beds, a dresser, and a chair. (But we had our own bathroom—which is not something you take for granted in Europe.)

We freshened up and then met my folks downstairs and went to have dinner in a nearby Italian restaurant. Kensington is a busy part of London and reminded me a little bit of the neighborhood in New York where we live: There were grocery stores and laundromats, things like that. I was so glad we were going to have Italian food, which is my absolute favorite. I could eat spaghetti every day of the week.

My parents ordered fish, which they almost always do, but Zoe and I ordered pasta.

"So, Zoe, what was your favorite of all the places we visited today?" my father asked, in his best professor's voice.

"The Tower of London," she said, without a hint of hesitation.

I gave her a sidelong glance.

"Ah, it's my favorite, too," Jeremiah said. "Nowhere else do you get that sense of history. So much has gone on within those walls."

"It's always been a bit gory for my taste. What do you think, Cory?" my mother asked.

"I think I agree with you, Mom."

"Let's face it: Everything that happened there was *so* depressing," she continued.

"Not really," Zoe interrupted.

"Oh?" Once again Zoe had snatched my father's rapt attention.

"I mean, look at the book that Sir Walter Raleigh wrote in the Tower. That was hardly depressing. And the Yeoman said that Raleigh's wife and son used to visit. Why, he even had servants! So that's proof of someone leading a perfectly normal existence there."

"I don't think you could call being locked up for twelve years normal, Zoe," my mother said quietly. "He *was* beheaded, you know."

"But everybody dies eventually. That's not important! I'm telling you, he was content ... almost happy. Really!"

My parents were staring at Zoe now, while I froze, my roll halfway to my mouth.

My father cleared his throat before he spoke. "And how do you know all this, Zoe?"

She hesitated for the first time, and *I* knew *she* knew she had forgotten where she was for a moment and come dangerously close to blurting out something like "Why, I *saw* him there, of course! He said to say 'Hi'!"

"I just have a feeling ..." she finally said, her voice trailing off lamely. But she looked shaky.

I put down my roll then because I was feeling shaky, too, and I wasn't sure I could chew and listen at the same time.

The waitress came with our food, and three of us began to eat ravenously. But Zoe just sat, staring at the checkered tablecloth with this really sad, faraway look in her eyes. I was afraid my parents would ask her what was wrong and start everything up again, so I shot her a look to try and snap her out of it. It worked because she looked down at her plate, as if she'd just noticed the huge mound of fettucine carbonara sitting there. And she picked up her fork—but then she seemed to change her mind and replaced it without saying a word.

While this was going on, I managed to consume an enormous plate of spaghetti and meatballs, and now I eyed Zoe's carbonara, which remained untouched.

"Aren't you hungry?" I asked.

"Not really. Do you want mine?" she said, pushing her plate in my direction.

I didn't eat the whole thing, honestly. I just ate enough so that when we got up to go to the ladies' room, I had trouble squeezing between the chairs.

Back at Mrs. Fairworthy's, while we got ready for bed, I began to think about the incident at the Tower again.

I was lying on the bed examining the wallpaper when Zoe came out of the bathroom.

"I want to ask you something," I said, sitting up and feeling suddenly serious. "Zoe, tell me what happened in the Tower today. Were you seeing shadows? Is that why you were saying those things about Sir Walter Raleigh?" She nodded. "What did you see?"

"He was writing at his desk. But more important than what I saw is what I felt. I don't know whether I can explain it to you, but there was this kind of aura in the room. As if the feelings that people had there years ago hung there still, and I could sniff them, like perfume. And what I sensed there was not exactly happiness, but contentment. Satisfaction, actually. I'm sure it was from writing the book."

"It's happening a lot now, isn't it?"

She sat down on the other twin bed then, nodding her head and looking absolutely miserable.

"Zoe, I think we have to talk about that picture. The one you've got hidden in the frame?"

She looked up at me with a mixture of fear and anger in her eyes, and her mouth seemed to set in a grim line, as if to say *I'm finished ever talking to you.*

"Why?" she said, narrowing her eyes the way she had in the hallway that night. "Why do you have to know?"

"Because it's all mixed up with what's happening to you. At least I think it is."

But she just shook her head. "It scares me too much, Cory."

"Zoe, if I'm the only one you've told, well, I'm going home soon and I think you need help."

"See? You *do* think I'm daft!"

"Stop it, of course not! I mean, help to figure out why this is happening to you. You can't just ignore it and pretend it's not there. Then your head *will* explode. I mean, wouldn't you like to get rid of those headaches?"

She nodded then, looking suddenly shy. "I wish you didn't have to leave, Cory. I really do."

I didn't know what to say. I was looking forward to going home. Not that England hadn't been interesting. But I missed Diane, and all my other friends, and the TV shows we watched, and the things we did together in the summertime. But before I left, I realized, I wanted to find out the truth about what was happening to Zoe. Part of it was my natural nosiness, I guess, but the other part was because I really, truly felt sorry for Zoe Mitchell. And if I was the only friend she had in the world, then I had a responsibility, didn't I?

She went over to the window and stood with her back to me, watching a city now lit by streetlamps. And she didn't turn around even when she began to speak.

"It was a summer day about two years ago. Gram and I had gone to the village for Gala Day. It's held in June, and all the people come out for games and a concert and stuff. And that year, it was my birthday, too. I remember at first Gram wasn't going to go, but I begged her, and since it was my birthday, she finally gave in. She even let me take my camera." She paused here as if she couldn't believe what she was going to say. "Anyway, I took some pictures, and then Gram took a couple of pictures of me. And when I got the pictures back, one of them came back the way you saw. I mean, it was me all right, standing outside the inn. Only everything else had changed. There were those two old men in the picture with me, wearing those real old-fashioned clothes, and it was still the inn, you could tell that—but the way it must have been about a hundred years ago.

"Anyway, it was right after what had happened at

Hampton Court, and I was so frightened. I figured I had done something bad to make the picture come out that way, so at first I hid it in my room. But I was afraid Gram would find it when we were cleaning out my drawers, so I got the idea of hiding it behind one of the other pictures. That was in a book I read once."

"Zoe, are you sure you don't know who the men are?"

"No. Should I?"

"I don't know. But there has to be a reason they're there. You're sure they're not relatives or something?"

"I don't think so. But—"

"What?"

"It's nothing important, I guess. But remember, Cory, I told you that sometimes things that have happened in a room a long time ago leave traces like shadows that I can see?" I nodded, urging her to go on. "Well, I've been thinking about it. And I think maybe that's what must have happened when Gram took my picture. I acted like a magnet, drawing the shadows out. The lines got blurred, and what was happening there years ago got all mixed up with what was happening right at that moment, and it came together in the picture. It could happen, don't you think?"

I wasn't sure at that moment if she truly believed or if she was pleading for me to reassure her.

I swallowed hard. "I guess so," I said, wishing I

could sound more convincing. It was dark out now, and we had switched on the lamp that sat on the small night table.

"You know, Cory, I've never talked this much to anyone."

"It's good to talk sometimes."

"But now we really must be friends because we share a serious secret."

"Zoe, I'm not sure you should keep it a secret anymore."

Her face wrinkled up the way it did the first time I'd seen her in the hallway. Now I recognized it as a look of suspicion and distrust. "What are you saying? You can't tell anyone—you promised!"

"I know, I know, calm down. What I'm saying is, maybe *you* should tell someone. Someone who would know about things like that. You can't keep it a secret forever."

"Why not?"

"Why would you want to? If it is truly a gift, there must be people who would know about that sort of thing. People who aren't like your grandmother."

She was quiet for a moment, like maybe she was thinking how nice it might be not to think you were daft all the time.

"How about your parents? *They* seem very nice."

"They *are* very nice."

"But do you think they'd think I'm a head case?"

"Gee, I honestly don't know. They *are* a lot like your grandmother."

We sat in silence for a moment. "We have to think of an older person who's not like any of them," I said.

"Bridget!" she cried suddenly, her eyes shining.

"You think?"

"Of course! I don't know why I didn't think of telling her before. She's perfect!"

And the more I thought about it, I had to agree with Zoe. Bridget Collins might be absolutely perfect.

Although we spent the train ride home on Sunday making our plans, I was afraid that maybe at the last minute Zoe might change her mind. But she didn't. The thought of the mighty Bridget as our ally seemed to give her new courage, and at nine o'clock the next morning she was waiting out by the silver mailbox.

"Have you got the picture?" I whispered, feeling wonderfully like Nancy Drew.

She nodded silently, as if it might be too dangerous to speak.

"Where'd you say we were going?" I asked.

"To the library. Where else?" she said, and we both giggled. It was the white lie I had used, and I admit to a little twinge of guilt. With someone like Cornelia Jessup, you had to make up stories, but I'd almost never had to lie to my parents. Maybe stretch the truth a little, but never actually *lie.*

"Did you find out where she lives?" I asked as we started down the road.

"Yes, I did: twenty-one Bank Street."

"How did you work that?"

"I told Gram that I wanted to send her a thank-you note for being so kind while she was at the house."

"Hey, not bad!" I said, feeling genuine admiration.

After reaching the village, Zoe and I turned down the side street to the little intersection where Bank Street began. The picture was in a cloth bag that hung over Zoe's shoulder, and as we began to hurry, she clutched it to her tightly.

"Are you sure she'll be there?" I asked.

"All I know is, she starts work at the inn at ten o'clock. So we should catch her before she leaves."

We slowed down as we reached Bank Street and began to scan the row of houses for the right number.

"Twenty-nine . . . twenty-seven . . . twenty-five . . . twenty-three . . . here it is!" Zoe cried as we approached a white cottage with green shutters and a thatched roof. Messy clumps of wild flowers crammed the small front yard, spilling over into the narrow path that led up to the front door.

"You go first," she said, shoving me ahead.

"Oh, no you don't! You know her better. And anyway, it's *your* picture."

We stood there for a moment arguing, and then just as Zoe was about to lift the old, tarnished knocker, the door opened and Bridget appeared in the doorway.

"Well, what have we here? Is it visitors I'd be having?"

"Hi," I said.

"We . . . we just stopped by."

"We were in the neighborhood," I added.

"Were you now? Well, come along," she said as she closed the door behind her and locked it with a key that she slipped into her pocket. "I don't mean to be rude not inviting you in, but you caught me just as I was going to work. So, we'll have to have our visit while we walk, 'cause it's late I am again and Mrs. Parks will have me head."

She started off briskly down Bank Street with us on either side, hurrying to keep up with her. She didn't seem at all surprised that we were there but started right in with comments about the weather and a neighbor's dog who was digging up her hollyhocks. We reached the corner and started up the hill toward the village. I looked over at Zoe. *Tell her now,* my look was trying to say. *We'll be in the square soon if you don't start talking!*

"Bridget, there's something I need to speak to you about," she said finally.

"What is it, girl? Go ahead."

"Uh, I don't know how to say it."

Zoe looked over at me frantically.

"Bridget," I said, coming to the rescue because I suddenly realized that it was probably easier for me to talk about it, "do you believe in ghosts?"

Zoe shot me a look that let me know she could have phrased it better, and I shot her a look that said, *Then why didn't you?*

Bridget never broke stride, and for a moment I thought maybe she hadn't understood me because she didn't say anything. Then, without looking at either of us, she spoke. "Which one of you has been seein' what?"

I felt myself let out a little gasp.

Then Zoe said, "It's me, Bridget, and I need your help."

Bridget stopped then and stared at Zoe. "This wouldn't be you pulling my leg now, would it?" Zoe shook her head quickly, and I think Bridget realized that Zoe had never been known for her great sense of humor. Then she turned to me. "Is it some kind of American joke, maybe?"

"No, Bridget, honest. *Do* you believe? Because strange things are happening to Zoe and I have to go back to the States and she has no one she can talk to about it."

There. That about said it all, I thought.

She started walking again.

"What about your granny? Didn't you tell her?"

"Oh, no, I can't. Gram wouldn't hear of such a thing. She'd think I was daft!"

From the expression on Bridget's face, I knew she was digesting this bit of information and realizing it was true enough. But we had come to the square, and Gerald, Owen, and Patsy were sitting on the steps leading to the pub.

"I've got to go to work, children. I'm sorry; I'd like to hear more."

"When could we meet you again?" I asked. Then, remembering a phrase I'd read in one of my mysteries, I added, "Time is of the essence!"

"Is it now?" she said with a smile. "I tell you what. If you don't tell a soul, I'll meet you in a little bit down in the vaults. It's me day to do the inventory, and there'll be no one to bother us down there. You can talk to your heart's content."

"Down in the vaults?" Zoe repeated in a shaky voice.

"Aye. You know the way, don't you? In back of the inn, by the snowball bush, you just go down those steps when no one's looking, and I'll meet you inside. Say, in half an hour?"

We nodded, and she hurried ahead and through the door of the pub, giving a big hello to Gerald and the others as she stepped by them.

Zoe started down toward the chemist's and I followed.

"Good idea," I said as we went inside. "We can browse around in here for awhile before we go over to the inn. I don't want to get stuck trying to explain to those kids why we're heading down to the vaults."

Zoe looked at me, and I knew something bad was coming because she had the same look on her face that I remembered from the band concert.

"Cory, I can't."

"Can't what?"

"Can't go down to the vaults. They're part of the inn. I haven't gone near there since the photograph!"

"But you have to," I said, in what I hoped was my most convincing tone, "if you want Bridget to help you."

"I know that and I want to, just . . . not *there.*"

"Zoe, I don't blame you for being afraid. I'd be afraid, too. But we have to go to the inn if you want to get rid of this, whatever it is. Just think: If we solve the puzzle, you won't ever have to be afraid again!" I waited a moment for this to sink in. "Wouldn't that be *wonderful?*" I added.

It must have worked because in half an hour she was right behind me as we slipped around the other side of the inn and found the flight of steps in back, right where Bridget had said.

She hesitated in the doorway, and I could actually hear her breathing, that's how loud it was.

"It'll be okay, Zoe, I promise you it will."

But even as I said it, I knew that it was a false

promise because I had no more idea of what would happen down there than she did.

We slipped through the door as quietly as we could and found ourselves at the top of a long, dark flight of stairs. The staircase was winding and steep and led down to an old cellar that had to be the place they called the vaults. To tell you the truth, I thought it was a pretty scary place even if you didn't have a date with a ghost.

There were wine racks against the wall and huge kegs and sacks piled in the corner. The ceiling was made of stone, like the walls, but it had heavy, ornate arches, as if this were the basement of a castle. It was cool and damp, with a smell I couldn't make out, except it smelled old.

Bridget was kneeling by the foot of the stairs examining something on a shelf. She stood when she heard our footsteps.

"So you found your way, did you now! Come on over here."

We followed her directions and settled ourselves on two small casks in the center of the room. There were rows and rows of bottles along the walls, and it seemed to be Bridget's job to count them or check the labels.

"What's that you're doing?" I asked.

"Taking inventory. And it's a dull job, it is. But we can't be running out of our customers' favorite brandy now, can we? So, what's this about ghosts? You go ahead and talk, and I'll be listening even though I might not seem to be. I've got to turn these old bottles over here so the sediment doesn't settle."

I nudged Zoe. "Go ahead," I said. "Tell her like you told me."

And she did, starting slowly and sounding scared at first, with the story of the private school and then the maze. Then she told about other times, things I hadn't heard. And finally she led up to what had happened at Bath and the Tower of London. But she didn't mention the picture. I guess she was saving that.

As Zoe talked, Bridget finished turning the bottles on the far wall and came and sat at the bottom of the steps. When Zoe had stopped talking, there was silence for a moment, and then Bridget looked over at us.

"You've got the sight all right, that's for sure," she said.

"The what?"

"The sight. It's a gift, Zoe, clear and simple, and nothing to be so upset about."

"Have you ever known anybody else who had this . . . gift?" I asked. Not that I was doubting her. But it occurred to me that maybe she was just trying to make Zoe feel better.

"Sure enough. Where I come from, it's not unusual at all. But it usually runs in families, on the mother's side. Did your mother not have it?"

Zoe shook her head. "I really don't know too much about her."

"Aye, of course. But your grandmother?"

"Oh, no, I *know* she doesn't. She says people will think I'm . . . I'm what's the word . . . *unstable.* That's why I never told anyone."

"Balderdash," Bridget said.

I was getting sore sitting on the cask because it had big, knobby nails on it, so I got up and started to look around while Zoe continued talking to Bridget. There were some things hanging on the wall by the stairs that I hadn't noticed before, and I wandered over to see what they were. There were some pieces of paper framed, like diplomas, only I know that's not what they were. And then there were a couple of photographs, and the first thing I thought of was that here were photographs that looked a lot like the one that was in Zoe's bag. They were grainy and brown, and the men—all the people in them were men—wore the same kind of suits as the men in the photograph with Zoe.

For a moment I thought *that's* why he looked familiar, the one with the blond beard wearing what looked like a captain's hat. I stared at the picture a moment longer: the same long nose, the same mustache.

I turned to Zoe excitedly. "Come here and look at this!" I said.

She came over, and I heard a little gasp.

"Who is this man?" I asked Bridget, pointing to the figure in the picture.

She was still sitting on the stairs with a ledger on her lap, and she looked up when I spoke.

"Him with the hat? That's Captain Parks."

"Who's Captain Parks?" I asked, feeling Zoe beginning to tremble beside me.

"Let's see now, he'd be Patsy and Owen's great-great grandfather, I think. Why do you ask?"

I looked at Zoe. "Show her." But she only stood there dumbly. "Zoë, you have to!"

She reached into the bag then and drew out the picture. But before she could hand it to Bridget, I stopped her.

"Tell her first, Zoe. Tell her how it happened."

So she did. She told about the Gala Day and how it was her birthday, too, and the fact that this was the first time her grandmother had used the camera that had belonged to her mother. Hearing it again, I began to realize how special it must have been. It wasn't just an ordinary picture after all. When she had finished, she handed the picture to Bridget.

For a moment Bridget just sat there, staring at the picture in her lap without saying anything. Then she blessed herself quickly.

"Saints preserve us."

"What d'you think, Bridget. What *is* it?" I asked.

She glanced up at us then, looking almost startled, as if she had forgotten for a moment that we were there.

"It's fair obvious what it is, child."

"What do you mean?" Zoe pleaded.

"It's a *message,* Zoe. That it is—a message, clear and simple."

"A what?" I said, feeling as confused as Zoe looked. "Who would be sending Zoe a message? And from where?"

"Who? That's what you'll have to be finding out. We know that Captain Parks is one of the men. Now, who is the other?"

Zoe shook her head. "I don't know."

"As for the other part of your question, Cory, the message is from the beyond." I felt a shiver going up my spine. For all our talk about ghosts, to have a grown-up say it out loud, just like that, made it true and terrifying. As if she sensed this, Bridget looked at Zoe Mitchell. "But you knew that, girl, didn't you?"

Zoe nodded. "I guess so."

"Of course you did. That's why you've been so scared."

The Olbourne library was much smaller than our library at home. In fact, the whole library could probably fit in the children's room of the one on Eighty-eighth Street that I go to. It was too small to be of use to people doing research, like my mother. That's why she had to go into Spindle. But this one was perfect for Zoe and me because it had something no other library had—the *Olbourne Chronicle*.

I had first seen the *Olbourne Chronicle* the day that Zoe brought me in to borrow some books. The huge, musty-looking book stood in a place of prominence on a stand near the entrance. Zoe told me it was the history of the village and its citizens since the beginning in 1219. I don't know about you, but I couldn't even imagine how old that is. And I didn't care. The only time we were interested in was about one hundred years ago. According to Bridget, that was the period that appeared in the picture. It was her idea that we might find out the identity of the other man from the *Chronicle*. Maybe he was someone else who had lived here then, maybe somebody important, like the mayor. Of course, if he was a visitor who just happened to be passing through Olbourne, we were out of luck.

I was out of luck anyway, I thought, glancing at my watch. I didn't have the heart to remind Zoe that I was leaving in the morning and my parents expected me to spend the afternoon with them, packing and getting ready to go. But it wasn't just Zoe; the thought of leaving without knowing the secret of the picture was unbearable. And so I hurried after her up the steps and across the threshold of the Olbourne Free Public Library.

"May I help you?" the librarian said in a cheerful voice when she saw us make a beeline for the *Chronicle* and start to lift the heavy, cracked leather cover. Then she recognized Zoe and came from behind the counter. "What is it you're looking for, Zoe?" she asked. "Maybe I can help."

Zoe swallowed hard. "We want to see some pictures of the village the way it was about a hundred years ago," she said. Her jaw was set, and her eyes held the other woman's steadily as she spoke. I thought how much Zoe had changed. Gone was the shy Zoe, the nasty Zoe, and in her place was a girl who didn't need me to speak up for her anymore. Maybe being told you had a gift (instead of being told you were daft) had something to do with it.

The librarian stepped up and carefully lifted the lid. "Let's see now, that would be right about here," she said, turning the pages until she was about three-quarters through the book. "What is it exactly that you were hoping to find?"

"Oh, just . . . uh . . ." Zoe began stuttering. (So maybe she still needed me a *little.*)

"Clothes!" I said, not knowing until I had blurted it out that that was what I was going to say.

"Clothes?" she repeated, her gray eyebrows knitting together behind her rimless glasses.

"You know, costumes. How they dressed in those days."

"Oh, I *see.* What is this for? Are you in a pageant, a play of some sort?"

"Yeah, that's right," I went on quickly.

"At a school? At this time of year?"

"Oh, uh, yeah. At the Spencer School. That's a summer school," I said. I was not to be shut up, obviously. Like a runaway train, the stupid answers just came roaring out of my mouth.

"Spencer School—where is that?"

"West Seventy-ninth Street," I said. "In New York City."

"In America," Zoe said, adding the final note to the wondrous tale I had just invented.

"Oh, I see. Well, there are pictures here of various members of the community. You can look through, but please be careful turning the pages."

"Of course," I said. How did she know I always turn down the corner of a page instead of using a bookmark?

The first couple of pictures were of houses; then there were a couple with men in shirtsleeves and suspenders clipping sheep, then some women standing outside a store. We had turned three pages when we saw the first picture of the pub, and we both got very excited. But the men standing outside weren't familiar. The captain wasn't even one of them. When we came to a page marked "Environs," we knew we were near the end, and Zoe let out a long, disappointed sigh.

"That's it, I guess," she said. "We'll probably *never* know."

"Don't say that!" I said, more to reassure her than because I had any real hope.

On the next page was written, in old-fashioned ink, *Rose Farm, 1887.*

"Look," I said excitedly, "here's your grandmother's house!"

"Great," she said, not sounding impressed.

"It's hardly changed at all. Except there's no door where we have one now. And the driveway's different." I turned the page and scanned the photographs, fascinated. There was a picture of a pretty woman in a big skirt, standing in the rose garden holding a parasol, and there were pictures of different rooms in the house, with all the funny old furniture. I had forgotten what Bridget had said: Rose Farm was originally the manor house. I guess that's why it deserved this special treatment.

"Cory, he's not in there!"

"I'm sorry, Zoe, really I am. But we haven't finished yet."

"But we've seen the pictures of the inn. Those are just pictures of Rose Farm."

"Maybe there's something afterward," I said, flipping the page quickly. But the next few pages had pictures from the turn of the century, of villagers celebrating the new year of 1900.

"We may as well go," she said miserably. "You have to get home and pack."

"Let me just finish," I said.

I was hoping to find a picture of my bedroom when another photograph caught my eye. It was taken in the back of the house, and there were two beautiful hunting dogs in the foreground, much like Daisy and Winston. A figure stood in the background with a shotgun under his arm and his hand in his pocket. He wore a hunting jacket and riding jodphurs and was unmistakably the lord of the manor. And unmistakably . . .

"Zoe! I found him!"

I was so excited that I forgot to lower my voice, and the librarian looked up.

"Is everything all right?" she asked, coming over.

"Oh, yes!" I said, starting to giggle. "Everything's

just great!" Zoe was peering over the book, studying his face intently.

"You're right," she said, barely breathing.

"Could you tell us who this is?" I asked.

She put her glasses on and studied the picture. "Why, that's Clive Dunbrook, the lord of the manor. The Dunbrooks were the family that owned Rose Farm for centuries, before Mrs. Jessup took over."

Zoe and I looked at each other, bewildered. This didn't bring us any closer to the truth.

"Did he have anything to do with the inn and Captain Parks?" I asked.

"I shouldn't think so. Captain Parks, why, I'm surprised you even know of him. He's not even in the *Chronicle.* A sea captain he was, just came home long enough to sire another brood—oh, I'm sorry," she said hastily. "Anyway, I hardly think they would have known each other." She closed the book carefully, as if sensing that we were through, and went back behind the desk. Then she turned as if she'd just thought of something. "Unless, of course, you count the fact that Lord Dunbrook was the captain's landlord."

"He was?"

"Of course he was. The Dunbrooks owned most of the village. Some of the villagers managed to buy their land from the manor. But as far as I know, the inn is still owned by the estate—by your grandmother, dear."

Zoe and I walked slowly down the steps of the library and out into the breezy English afternoon. We didn't speak until we had settled ourselves in back of the pub on the steps leading down to the vault. Gerald and the others were out by the fountain, but they wouldn't see us here and we could mope in peace.

"What do we do now?" Zoe asked.

"I don't know. Somehow I thought that if we knew who the men were, it would all fall into place. But it doesn't. It's like we have two pieces of the puzzle, but that's all. There's a lot more holes left."

"And you're leaving tomorrow."

"Well," I said, "you can always write me about it."

"About *what?* You expect me to go around the village showing the photograph and asking people questions? Either I'll be locked up as a nut or, if they believe me, I'll be a . . . a—"

"Curiosity," I offered hopefully.

"Thanks."

"We have to talk to Bridget."

"She said she'd be off at four. What time is it now?"

"Ten of."

I had told my parents I was taking a last look at the village and would be home by noon. I'm surprised they didn't have Scotland Yard out looking for me.

The door to the vaults opened, and Bridget

slipped out, closing it firmly behind her. "I thought I heard you. What did you discover?"

"He's Lord Dunbrook, lord of the manor!" Zoe squealed, as if she'd suddenly lost her mind and was excited that she'd posed with a celebrity.

"Zoe," I wanted to say, "it doesn't really count when the celebrity's been dead for a hundred years."

"Is that a fact!" Bridget said, sounding impressed.

"But it doesn't really help us much, does it?" I said.

"Maybe if we knew when the picture was taken, it would help. At least that would be another part of the puzzle," Zoe said.

"Wait," Bridget cried, "I might be able to help you. Let me see it again." She studied the picture for a moment without saying a word. "You two stay here." And she was off in a flash. In a few moments, she came back up the steps. "Eighteen eighty-seven or thereabouts."

"How do you know?"

"Because it's a known fact that sea captains were only home every three years or so. Those pictures downstairs have dates on the back, and the one where he looks the most like he did in your picture is dated April 1887. He was a handsome devil, I have to give him that."

"That makes sense because the pictures in the *Chronicle* of Rose Farm were from 1887, too."

"So now, what do we know?" Bridget began. "Something happened in 1887 between the captain and Lord Dunbrook, and it was something that they're trying to tell Zoe about. And the only connection that we know of is that Lord Dunbrook owned the inn."

"That doesn't tell us much. Are there any other records around, Bridget?"

"Let's see. Wait a minute, there's the ledgers. Of course! I should have thought of that right away. The Dunbrook ledgers! They give the history of the manor—of the whole village, actually. Mainly it's the price of livestock and that sort of thing, but I know there's private things in there, too. Actually, they should have been given to the library long ago."

"Why weren't they?" Zoe asked.

"I don't rightly know. It *was* a bit queer, now that I think of it. When the last of the Dunbrooks passed on, the village asked to go through them things. They're all stored in the basement of your grandmother's house, but she wouldn't hear tell of it. You'd think they was contagious the way she carried on, I remember. Wouldn't let anyone go near the stuff."

Bridget frowned then, as if a new and disturbing idea had just occurred to her. Then she cocked her head to one side and stared at Zoe intently.

"What is it, Bridget?" Zoe asked. "What's wrong?"

"Nothing, Zoe, nothing. Just maybe it's not *you* the message is meant for, after all."

"I've been frantic! Where on earth have you been?"

"Hi, Mom, sorry I'm a little late. You remember Bridget—"

"A little late! What's wrong? Something's wrong, isn't it?"

"Calm down, Mom. Nothing's wrong. I'm sorry if you were worried."

"You're sorry if we were— Cory, this is not your kind of behavior!"

Bridget, Zoe, and I were standing in the driveway, our race home blocked by the appearance of my mother in the doorway of the house as we approached. I'd never seen her so upset. Back home in New York City she never seemed to worry, but here in Olbourne she was a wreck, and I couldn't understand it. What did she think could happen?

Sorry I'm late, Mom, but I was mugged by a sheep.

It took a little coaxing to get Bridget to come home with us. Not that she wasn't as anxious as we were to get to the bottom of this, but she would have waited until tomorrow, and by tomorrow *I* would be on my way back to America.

"So? Where have you been all day?"

"Just saying good-bye to people," I lied, keeping my fingers crossed so it didn't count.

"I didn't realize you had that many friends," my mother said in the tone of voice she always uses when she wants *me* to know that *she* knows I'm stretching the truth. But that wasn't important now. What was important was getting past my mother and into Cornelia Jessup's house with Zoe and Bridget. But she wasn't in on our plan, obviously. "Go right upstairs and start getting your things organized, Cory. We're having dinner with Cornelia tonight, and I want you to be all packed before then."

I looked frantically at Bridget, but I could tell by her expression that she wasn't going to be able to help me out.

"Could I just go in with Zoe for a minute?" I asked. "She wants to show me something."

"No. I'm sorry, Cory, but I want you to go upstairs immediately. You can see Zoe at dinner."

Zoe's eyes grew wide as I threw her a look over my shoulder and went inside. As I deliberately slammed the door behind me, I bumped into my father, who was coming out of the laundry room with a bunch of socks in his hand.

"Well, well, the prodigal daughter. Your mother's really had her knickers in a twist over you today, young lady. Where've you been?"

I sighed loudly, very loudly, to let him know how tired I was of people making a federal case out of me being a little late getting home. "Just around," I said, stomping up to my room.

Once I got there, I pulled my duffle bag out of the closet and placed it on top of the bed. Then I threw my body down next to it. It wasn't as if I had this huge wardrobe to pack! Parents could be so unreasonable. Now I wouldn't be there when they confronted Cornelia. I wanted to watch her squirm as they wrung a confession out of her black heart. (All right, so maybe she wasn't the worst person in the world, but she was a pain, and the thought of her up against Bridget sounded like more fun than a rock concert.) I heard my mother's footsteps on the stairs and looked up to see her standing in the doorway.

"What is going on, Cory?"

"I was just resting for a moment," I said, and I jumped up and started pulling out the dresser drawers.

"Don't play innocent with me, young lady; that's not what I mean and you know it! There's a terrible row going on in Cornelia's, and while I certainly wasn't eavesdropping, I couldn't help but hear your name being bandied about."

"Really?" I said, suddenly pleased. "What were they saying?"

"I'm not sure. Cornelia is very upset, I know that. The other two seem to be pleading with her about something, or trying to convince her of something, and you are in on it. Now, what's it all about? Obviously this is why you were gone all day."

"Mom, let me go downstairs."

"Not until you're all packed."

I got so mad that without really thinking about it I just turned and, in four perfectly executed moves, dumped the contents of the three drawers *and* the closet into my duffle bag.

"There. *Now* can I go?"

My mother got that tight look around her mouth that usually acts as a red flag, warning me that I've gone too far. But I couldn't worry about that; I had to get downstairs and see what was going on. She didn't budge from her place in the doorway.

"We are guests here, Cory, and if you've made trouble for Cornelia, it would be most embarrassing. Now you may go downstairs when you tell me what is going on."

This last was said in the singsong teacher's voice that I absolutely hate. I took a deep breath. "Okay, here goes. Zoe Mitchell has this 'gift' where she can see things in places—things and people that were there a long time ago. And one day a couple of years ago, Cornelia took Zoe's picture with Rachel's camera, and two people who've been dead for a hundred years popped up in it. But now we know who the two people are: They're Captain Parks and Lord Dunbrook, and they're trying to get a message through. Only Bridget thinks the message isn't for Zoe after all, but for her grandmother. *Now* can I go?"

The good thing about telling my mother everything like that was that it left her speechless—I mean, literally standing there looking dumber than I've ever seen her look—which allowed me to slip by and race down the stairs.

I didn't know whether she was following me or not, but I went right over to the kitchen door, bold as brass (as Miss Cotten used to say in third grade), and when nobody answered my knock, I opened the door and went on through.

The dining room was empty; so was the living room. But I knew they were in the house because I could hear them. I stood still for a moment and realized that the muffled sound of raised voices was coming from their kitchen, and as I hurried on through, the voices became louder and more distinct.

"I don't believe any of this. It's a fraud, it's a trick, and I won't have such deceit under my roof."

"What are you saying, Gram? It's me, Zoe, you're

talking about! How can it be a trick? And why would I *do* that?"

I peeked around the doorway. The three of them were standing at an open door that seemed to lead down to the basement where the ledgers were kept. Zoe was holding the picture, which she'd obviously shown to her grandmother, and Cornelia Jessup looked really upset. Her hands were up to her face as if she was crying. "Please don't do this, Bridget. There's nothing to find in those musty old books."

"If you don't want to look, Mrs. Jessup, you can stay here. I'm not wanting to upset you. But it's you or Zoe here; you do understand that now, don't you? She's been having these headaches something fierce. And you've been telling the poor child she's going daft. Sure and that would give anybody headaches."

"I didn't mean any harm."

"I know you didn't, Gram. But don't you see, if we can examine the ledgers for 1887, maybe we can find out what it is they're trying to tell us."

"I can't look at them again," the older woman said finally.

"Then you've seen them? Tell us, Gram, please!"

"If you'll just give me a moment, I will. I promise. I guess it's time."

She turned to go back into the parlor and spotted me in the doorway.

"You might as well come, too, Cory. I understand you've been in on this all along."

We settled ourselves in the parlor, and I thought of my parents right on the other side of the wall, and what they must be thinking, and I wondered if I'd be grounded for life when this was finally over. But it would be worth it.

"I suppose that Bridget may be right," Cornelia began. "Maybe it is a gift, if one is willing to accept it as such. The truth is, Zoe, I couldn't. It frightened me too much, and it was against everything I had ever believed in."

"*You,* Gram? You had it, too?"

Cornelia Jessup took a deep breath, her chest under her purple cardigan rising and falling with a great effort.

"It began for me much later than it has for you, Zoe. It was at a site in Luhan, in the Valley of the Nile. We had just entered a chamber to catalog some of our findings when I got the strangest sensation. At first, it was just a feeling like being lightheaded, a bit dizzy. Then I began to smell this strong, acrid odor. I knew immediately what it was. I recognized it as a substance the Egyptians used in embalming their dead. But there was no way I should have been able to smell it there after all those centuries. I remember that I had an aide with me, Bonnie, and I asked her if she smelled anything peculiar and she said no. For me, the stench was so overpowering that I began to retch and had to leave the tomb. And that was the beginning. I would visit a site and touch something and know who it had been made for, who had used it. A kind of vibration would go right through my body. Rachel was a small child at the time, and when she was with me, I began to sense that it was happening to her, too. She tried to tell me about it, but I hushed her up. Just as I tried to hush you, Zoe. But it didn't do any good. I don't know why I didn't learn."

Cornelia got a distant look in her eyes and seemed to be distracted for a moment. But then she continued.

"Anyway, it just kept getting stronger. When I began to see shapes and shadows, I feared for my sanity, so I retired from fieldwork, thinking I would be safe in academia. I concentrated on research and the lecture hall. And it seemed to be all right for a time, but while it may have abated in me, it was still very much a part of Rachel's life. Maybe she was able to accept it as a gift—who knows? We were very different, she and I. As soon as she was out of school, she took off with her camera and never looked back. Eventually, of course, it began with me again, and I had to avoid certain halls, certain manuscripts. And then . . . then the accident happened . . ." Cornelia hesitated but went on. "Now I had the excuse I needed to give it all up. With Zoe to care for, I retired and bought Rose Farm. Here in the country, with my dogs and my roses, I thought I would find peace. But I guess it wasn't to be."

"What happened, Gram?"

"It started about five years ago when members of the village council came and asked to examine the ledgers. They mentioned something about doing a history of the village, but I think it was just sheer nosiness. I hadn't even known the ledgers were down there. But of course, when I went down to look, that's when it happened."

"*What* happened, Gram?" Zoe asked.

"I saw someone. He was hovering over in the corner. I was still steeped in my grief . . . I thought I was hallucinating! I mean, Bridget, God help me, rational people don't see things like that. They *don't.* It can't really happen!"

Nobody said anything for a few moments. Then Cornelia continued.

"I guess I panicked. I told them that I couldn't find any ledgers, and they left."

"But that wasn't the end of it, was it?" Bridget asked. "What happened after that?"

"I received a visit from Mr. and Mrs. Parks. Supposedly they were just welcoming me to Olbourne. But it soon became clear they had an ulterior motive."

Bridget spoke again. "And what would that have been?"

"Well, as I say, they came to see me, fawning

something dreadful, how I was such a great lady, all that kind of rubbish. Anyway, they told me quite a tale. A bit of Parks family folklore, handed down from one generation to the next."

"What did they tell you, Gram?"

"They told me that one day Lord Dunbrook's young grandson was riding through the village and his horse was startled by a stray cat. He bolted and would have thrown the boy, but Captain Parks happened to be leaving the inn at the time, and he jumped up, grabbed the reins, and brought the horse under control. And the next day or so, Captain Parks told his wife, Lord Dunbrook paid a visit to the inn and promised the captain that in gratitude for his having saved the boy's life, he was going to deed the inn over to the Parks family. It's quite a valuable piece of property, you know. But it seems the lord passed on himself not long after, without having made it official. There were no witnesses to the incident except the child, and he knew nothing of the subsequent visit. Why, there was no one who could recall even seeing Lord Dunbrook with Captain Parks, so when the captain approached the heir sometime after the funeral, he was turned out as a scoundrel. But he recorded it in his diary, and ever since, each Parks heir who has lived there has looked on the manor with loathing, feeling somehow cheated, I suppose."

"But what did they expect from you?" Zoe asked.

"They wondered if I had seen anything in the ledgers, which it seems included diaries kept of comings and goings on the farm. They assumed, I suppose, that the old man might have recorded such an incident and his intention of giving the inn to the Parks family. Well, I told them quite honestly that I was unaware of any diaries. And that was the truth—I had never seen any. I mean, obviously, they didn't have a leg to stand on or they would have taken to the courts, wouldn't they?"

There was silence for a moment and then Zoe spoke.

"So my mother had this gift, too."

Cornelia looked up at Zoe then, and her eyes were filled with tears. I had to look away. "She was a wonderful photographer, you know. Your mother had a marvelous eye."

Zoe smiled then, and I wondered if this was the first time the older woman had ever said something kind to her about her mother.

"We must look at the ledgers, Gram. You see that, don't you?"

"I suppose we do."

"You can stay up here, Mrs. Jessup. I'll go with the girl," Bridget said.

"No." Zoe got up and stood by her grandmother's chair. "Gram, I think this is something we should do together. It will be all right if we're together; I know it will be."

I got up then because I knew it was time to leave. Whatever would happen downstairs when they opened the ledger marked 1887 was between Zoe and her grandmother. It was a gift, all right, and it was special, but right then I knew it was also kind of private.

"Pass the muffins, please."

Even though we'd had a wonderful, giddy farewell dinner last night at Cornelia's, I hadn't eaten very much in the excitement, and now I was famished as my mother ladled out a big breakfast to start us on our trip.

"More sausage, Cory?"

"Please!"

"Well, this has turned out to be quite an adventure for you, young lady, hasn't it?" my father said.

"Yep. I think I'll do a term paper on paranormal phenomena when I get back."

"Oh, so you know all the terminology now, do you?"

"Sure."

"Thank God you managed to convince Zoe to stop hiding that picture. Think of the damage that was being done to both Cornelia and her granddaughter," my mother said.

"I wonder if old Cornelia's ever going to be really happy about it," I said.

"Perhaps not. But if she'll just let Zoe be herself, that's the most important thing! Maybe then the poor child will stop having those headaches. And I hope Cornelia lets her go back to the Kensington school."

"I think she will," my father said. "Zoe obviously needs to be around her peers. And speaking of that, I imagine she'll be more popular with the children in the village, too, once the inn has been deeded over to the Parks family."

"Isn't that neat? I guess they can really use the money. Does this mean they'll be rich, like Cornelia Jessup?"

"Hardly, Cory. But it means they won't have any rent to pay, and they'll be landowners. It'll be quite a step up for them socially, as well."

"I wonder what Cornelia's going to tell them?"

"Oh, probably that she came upon the ledgers and accidentally found this entry in August 1887. It's a good thing that the old man made note of what happened when he did. But if it hadn't been for this gift of Zoe's, the whole thing might never have been discovered."

"I still can't figure out why Cornelia was so afraid of it."

"Well, paranormal phenomena are very controversial, Cory. A lot of people just don't believe that those who have passed on, as they say, can communicate with those of us who are still hanging around down here."

"Do *you?*"

My father glanced at my mother and began to butter his toast rather violently.

"I don't know, Cory. If you had asked me that a month ago, I would have given you a straight no. But now I don't know what to think. I am, after all, a man of science."

"But you deal in this sort of thing all the time. You and Mom and Cornelia Jessup. That's why I can't understand why she didn't accept it."

"We deal—whatever are you talking about, Cory?"

"Well, look at it this way," I began. "All you archaeologists are trying to do, really, is find out about people who lived centuries ago, right?"

"Well, yes."

"Only you do it by digging up the houses they lived in and the dishes they used—things like that. But just think about it. With a gift like Zoe's, you get to meet the people themselves. Bingo! It's a kind of shortcut, you know?"

There was silence for a moment, and my parents looked at each other and at me, and then my mother said, "Cory, could you remember to bring that rather original mind of yours home with you? And maybe into the classroom this year?"

I grinned. "Okay," I said.

We cleaned up the kitchen, and my parents started upstairs to get their bags. Then we would be off to the airport again with old Jeremiah behind the wheel. Talk about scary!

As I started to follow them, there was a light tap on the kitchen door and when I opened it, Zoe was standing there, much like her grandmother had so many times in the last few weeks.

"I want to give you something," she said, handing me a wrapped package.

"A present! But I didn't get you anything."

She shook her head. "It's not really a present. It's just something I want you to take to America with you. Sort of a souvenir."

I tore off the wrapping, and it was the same kind of frame as *the* photograph, and for a moment my heart gave a little leap. Then I realized that it was the picture Bridget had taken of us on Golden Top.

I nodded dumbly and we hugged, and then I took the picture up to my room.

As I threw the last couple of things into my bag, I started to feel really sad all of a sudden because I realized that I might never see Zoe Mitchell again. But then I began to think about how when you're grown up you get on airplanes and go and visit people all the time and it's no big deal. And even if we don't see each other for a long time, she can become one of those once-in-a-lifetime friends, like my parents have. My mother says those are the friends that you hardly ever see but you never, ever forget. And you tell your kids great stories about them all the time.

When I was all ready, the last thing I slipped into my duffle bag was the picture, and as I wrapped it in a sweater to protect it, I thought I caught a glimpse, just a quick maybe-I'm-mistaken kind of glimpse of a slit in the back. A very special kind of slit—the kind that would make a really neat hiding place. But I shoved it into my bag without another look. I wasn't sure, and I didn't want to check. And maybe I won't, not for years and years and years.

Somehow it seems more fun that way.